To K...

with ....

love from

Looking for Home

Jane

First published in 2016 by Beggar Books

Copyright © Jane Corbett 2016

A CIP catalogue record for this book
is available from the British Library

ISBN: 978-1-910852-92-7
eISBN: 978-1-910852-93-4

Cover image and design by Jamie Keenan
Typeset by www.headandheartpublishingservices.com

Looking for Home

Jane Corbett

Part One

Paris, January 1st 1927
Merline

Head down, Merline strode the left bank of the river, seeing and hearing nothing. When she reached the Pont d'Austerlitz, she crossed the bridge to the other side and resumed her walk along the opposite bank in the direction she had come. Her journey had one purpose, to annihilate through the numbing rhythm of her footsteps all thoughts of the day to come. Rilke, the love of her life, was dead. Tomorrow, January 2nd, he would be buried in Switzerland and she was not invited.

For five years, the most precious of her life, they had loved one another in the time left over from the exigencies of his work. He had loved many women but she knew herself to be the greatest object of his passion, even if truth forced her to acknowledge that what they'd shared existed more in the imagined than the real world. It was she who'd found his haven, the Château de Muzot, in which he'd spent his last, most settled years, with the peace so necessary for his great work. She had made it habitable with her own hands, labour that made her proud, though in the eyes of his rich and powerful friends it merely confirmed her menial status.

For years they had done their best to deny her existence, and in the end they'd triumphed. Only her son, Balthus, the young acolyte who showed such remarkable promise as a painter, had been invited to the funeral. Such acknowledgement from those who would become the future patrons of his work made her proud but did little to soften the bitterness of her own exclusion. And that was as nothing to her grief.

Berlin, 1993
Eli

On July 13th Eli delivered her first commissioned article to the London based magazine *Art Today*. This time the copy would go out under her own name. The pay cheque coincided with her thirtieth birthday and to celebrate she decided to spend a few days with her friend Bill in Berlin. They'd been students together at the Courtauld Institute and he was currently working as an architect on one of the multiple projects transforming an isolated bohemian backwater into the modern capital of a united Germany. As this was her first time in Berlin, Bill took her on a tour of the city.

The place was unlike anywhere else she'd been and hugely exciting. Busy streets ran alongside patches of wasteland, and fragments of road, untouched since 1940s bombings, suddenly petered out, leading nowhere. The earth heaved under a myriad excavations and up above cranes criss-crossed the horizon like parts of a giant Meccano set. Amid such uprooting anything seemed possible.

As they moved on from the New National Gallery, Bill pointed out a couple of old embassies on the far side of the street, derelict for fifty years because, he explained, the countries they belonged to had ceased to exist. Their walls were still pockmarked with bullet holes and in a garden where once elegantly dressed people had taken tea on the lawn, a herd of goats grazed peacefully on tall heads of thistles.

Further on they came to a huge empty space that before the war had been one of the city's busiest squares. Bulldozers were clearing away scrub and rubble, untouched for half a century. As they left the viewing platform that showed the layout of the projected development, Eli stumbled on a newly exposed grating half-buried in the earth. A flight of steps lead down into the ground and an empty cigarette packet lay in the dust. She could just make out the writing on the packet – 'Capstan Full Strength'. It was, she realised, the entrance to an old U-Bahn station, and time concertinaed itself in a rush. A young man in uniform tossed away the empty pack as he hurried down the steps to catch the last train that would ever leave that platform before the bomb fell that annihilated it.

The city threw up many such images, moments in which the past jerked suddenly to life like the hands of some crazy clock lurching senselessly back and forth. One never knew what twisted relic or perfectly intact fragment might present itself in all its incongruity, such as the elegant nineteenth-century house that stood alone in the flattened desert of Potsdamer Platz, waiting to be entombed within the steel and glass to come like a fly in amber.

A few days after her arrival they were invited to meet up with friends at a small restaurant in Schöneberg, and it was here she met Gunter and fell in love. They were seated next to each other at the end of a long table. At first, amid all the lively talk he paid her little attention. Bill pointed him out as a well known filmmaker and not wanting to seem too impressed, her manner towards him was deliberately cool. Halfway through the meal, he laughed at a remark he overheard her make to her neighbour on the other side, and after that they fell into conversation. They were still talking when the party broke up around midnight.

The following day he called her at Bill's to ask if she'd like supper at his flat.

'Why his place and not a restaurant? Is he a known seducer?' she asked.

Bill laughed. 'Why're you so suspicious? You should be flattered.'

She blushed like a schoolgirl. 'He's at least ten years older than me.'

'He's in his prime. Anyway, I thought women liked mature men.'

Kreuzberg, where Gunter lived, was a poor, largely Turkish neighbourhood that until recently had cowered in the shadow of the Wall. Coming out of the U-Bahn onto the main street, Eli was struck by its ugliness. A few dusty trees lined a wide street but no flowers or bushes brightened up the central reservation. A row of shops sold shoddy goods it was hard to imagine anyone buying, and further on there was a seedy strip club and a slot-machine arcade where listless youths, mainly Turkish, had taken up residence. From the doorway of a small supermarket a group of punks, with their dogs and cans of lager, shouted abuse at passers-by.

Eli turned into a side street that ran along the canal and the scene transformed. A busy Turkish market sold everything from trinkets and clothes to exotic foods, and further on a couple of cafés were packed with lively people.

Gunter lived on the top floor of an old apartment house overlooking the canal, one of several that had survived the blitz. Like most old Berlin houses it had a square, protruding bay that ran the height of the building, and was built around an inner courtyard with a large sycamore tree. She pressed the bell and was buzzed in. There was no lift so she took the staircase that smelt pleasantly of beeswax and old wood. She had to pause for breath a couple of times before she reached the fourth floor.

Gunter was waiting. He greeted her with a friendly kiss on the cheek and welcomed her into the flat. The living room was large with a high ceiling and big windows. An Afghan rug and a few items of stylish modern furniture created a pleasantly uncluttered feel. At the far end there was a desk piled high with papers and a wall of bookshelves. Photographs had been Blu-Tacked to the adjacent wall, mostly of cities by night. A saxophone stood in one corner and on the shelves between the books there were small collections of stones and fragments of bone, worn smooth by time or water.

Gunter poured them both a glass of wine.

'D'you play?' she asked, pointing at the sax.

'I used to. Not any more. I leave it there to remind myself there's more to life than making films.'

He handed her a glass. 'I hope you're hungry. The food's almost ready.'

He led the way to the kitchen. There was a window looking into the courtyard and space enough for a big table and six chairs. He gestured her to take a seat, whilst he finished his preparations for the meal. Awkwardly self-conscious in a way she hadn't been since adolescence, she searched for some easy remark to break the ice but none came to her.

'So, how d'you find Berlin? It's your first time, I believe.' He spoke without turning round, which was a relief. She didn't want him to look at her till she'd regained some self-possession.

'Yes. The city seems to be changing before one's very eyes. It's an extraordinary experience!'

'Like most Berliners, I find it rather depressing. Before it belonged to artists and old people. Now it's being turned into just another temple of capitalism. Rents go up, Starbucks and fancy restaurants replace the old clubs and bars. Soon only politicians and tourists will want to live here.'

'To a stranger it seems full of life.'

He took a bowl of squid that had been marinating out of the fridge and tossed them into a frying pan. 'You're right. I'm just an old cynic! I hope you like these fish? They need eating at once or they go rubbery.'

'I come from an island. I was brought up on fish!'

After an attempt at speaking German, they changed to English and the conversation grew easier. It frustrated her that most Germans were fluent in English in a way that made her efforts to speak their language hopelessly laborious.

The squid was delicious and she downed the glass of Chablis he poured her too fast.

'You obviously like to cook.'

'When I have someone to cook for.'

'I admire anyone who does. I live mostly off cottage cheese and takeaways.'

'Then we're a perfect match!' His smile was disarming and she began to relax.

He cleared the plates away for the next course and asked casually, 'What about Bill?'

'What about him?'

He placed a dish of black pasta coloured with fragments of red pepper and chilli and a bowl of salad onto the table.

'You mean is he domesticated? Not as far as I've noticed. Like most Englishmen.'

'No. I meant how long have you known him?'

He helped them both to pasta. If she was not mistaken, he was asking whether she and Bill were an item.

'We did our MAs together at the Courtauld in London. When I heard he was working in Berlin I got in touch and asked if he had a spare bed.'

Bit by bit the sense of wellbeing from the delicious food and the wine she'd drunk loosened her tongue. Despite their differences in age and experience Gunter was easy to talk to, as though they shared a natural kinship. He spoke about his struggle to raise money for the film he was planning, a documentary about Malawi. Then he turned the subject to her.

'You're a journalist, I believe?'

'I work for a magazine called *Art Today*. The editor hired me after reading my dissertation on the painter Balthus. I'm still more or less on trial.'

'So, who are the current British artists that interest you?'

She thought for a moment. Most of them were young with as yet little reputation. 'There are a few, relatively unknown. Art in Britain right now is too much in thrall to fashion and the market, especially America. In Germany things seem freer.'

'Yes and no. Pretentiousness can be mistaken for serious-ness. But I agree. German artists have a genuine desire to ex-periment.' He paused to refill her glass. 'With film we're more conventional or no one will pay to watch it. At least, that's my excuse for not taking risks I probably should.'

She asked about life in Berlin before the fall of the Wall and he told her how in the 1970s when he first came there to avoid being drafted into the army, living was so cheap that money had little importance.

'Half the refugees of Europe found haven here. Russians touted their war medals and old watches on street corners for pfennigs. Now they're opening smart galleries selling icons for thousands of dollars under the auspices of a well organised mafia. In those days we got whatever we needed to furnish our communal flat from what people put out on the pavement one Sunday a month for passers-by to help themselves.'

When at length Eli looked at her watch, it was almost midnight.

'I must go. I hope I haven't kept you too late. I know you have work tomorrow.'

'I feel a lot less tired than before you arrived.'

'That's nice!'

'It's a way of asking if you'll stay a little longer? If you're not expected back.'

'What about the U-Bahn? When does that stop?'

'If it closes, I'll drive you.'

She hesitated, sensing where this was leading. She wasn't

in the habit of jumping into bed on a first date. In fact it was some time since she'd jumped into bed at all. But she had the impression his invitation wasn't merely routine and if she refused was unlikely to be repeated. There was no point in being coy.

'I'd better give Bill a call. He might think something's happened to me.'

'Good!' he said, and poured them both another glass of wine.

For the rest of the week they were rarely apart. Making love with Gunter was a completely new experience. He made her feel desired as no man had ever done and in response she gave herself to him without reserve. When she woke in the night, she studied his face in the faint glow from the street lamp, memorising every detail, too happy to sleep. She breathed in the smell of his skin and mown grass scent of his hair then, reaching for his hand in the dark, laid it on her breast until half-waking he stirred and drew her closer into his embrace. His touch ignited in her an insatiable desire.

She did her best not to think of how soon she would be leaving. But too quickly the time came and she was back in the loneliness of her London flat. She told herself it was a good thing she'd left Berlin before infatuation subjected her entirely, but she found it impossible to concentrate or to settle to anything. She spent fruitless hours daydreaming and trying not to pick up the phone. Awake for much of the night she nodded off in the cinema, and going out with friends bored her because she refused to talk about the one thing on her mind. At times she found herself overcome by emotion as if the rational judgement that had been her guiding light had evaporated, leaving her helpless in the face of her obsession. It was a situation that couldn't be allowed to continue.

Paris, 1993
Eli

Relief came a couple of weeks later when Michael, her editor at the magazine, was laid low with a bout of sciatica and offered her the chance to go to Paris in his stead. The assignment was to review an important Poussin exhibition that was about to open there, exactly the distraction she needed.

'You might, if you're lucky, get to see your hero at close quarters. It's a big occasion and if he's in Paris he's bound to be there.'

'You mean Balthus?'

He nodded. 'I doubt you'll get the chance to speak to him. His entourage will see to that. Still, better be prepared on the off chance.'

'I will!'

She decided to go by ferry and train. She loved trains and it would allow her more time with the poet Rilke's letters, part of her research into Balthus' origins. From them she'd just discovered that Merline, the last and perhaps greatest of all Rilke's loves, was Balthus' mother. Unlike Rilke's other women she lacked both fortune and breeding, and he often made reference to her enforced nomadic existence and the desperate money worries she and her children endured during the period surrounding the Great War. He wrote to her mainly in French, though both their first languages were German. He even declared a bitter hatred of the German language that as a boy growing up in Prague had been the mark of his superiority. Only in French, he said, did he feel free to express his real thoughts. Eli found it hard to imagine what could make someone, especially a poet, reject their mother tongue.

As a student she'd been drawn to Balthus' work through his illustrations for Emily Brontë's *Wuthering Heights*. It was a favourite novel and these drawings seemed perfectly to capture the spirit of its frustrated, savage longing. In one of her favourite drawings Heathcliff is seated in a chair, whilst the nurse brushes Cathy's hair. Cathy, dressed only in a light slip, ignores him and he looks away from her in a manner of seeming indifference that does nothing to disguise the barely suppressed violence of his jealousy. What especially intrigued her was that Balthus had drawn himself as Heathcliff.

As a girl she'd read and reread the novel, seated, weather permitting, in the great cedar tree where their father had built a tree house. Open to the winds that blew from the north, it was such a place as Brontë's wilful heroine might herself

14

have chosen had she lived in the West Midlands instead of the Yorkshire Moors. There Eli revelled undisturbed in overheated fantasies about that fearful upstart Heathcliff, forgiving his cruelty in the spirit of 'to understand all is to forgive all' and Cathy's great cry of love, 'I am Heathcliff!'

After the discovery of 'Wuthering Heights', she'd sought out other paintings by Balthus – disturbing images of dreamy girls, thwarted young men and malign cats, that haunted her dreams. One of her tutors at the Courtauld argued strongly against her choice of him for her dissertation, claiming that he was an old-fashioned figurative painter, indifferent to modernism and little more than a sophisticated pornographer. She disagreed fiercely. It was true his work expressed a sensuality that at times bordered on the prurient. But even at their most extreme she found nothing gratuitous in his images. Rather an honesty that exposed the savage nature of youth's desire. He was in addition a remarkable craftsman, with a unique way of building up layer upon layer of paint to create a fresco-like quality through which the light magically diffused in a manner reminiscent of the early Italian masters. No one in the twentieth century, she declared, could paint light like he could.

Arriving in Paris she made a brief stop at the hotel to drop off her bag, then straight to the Grand Palais where the exhibition was being held. She entered the great salon and was at once overwhelmed by its magnificence and the formidable presence of so many glitterati. They were dressed with the uniform chic and good taste only Paris could produce. At the centre of the room a group of people were gathered around a tall, distinguished-looking elderly man and she took a sharp intake of breath. It was Balthus.

It was clear from the attention of those surrounding him that the presence of Count Balthasar Klossowski de Rola, as he liked to be known, was as significant as the paintings that adorned the walls. He'd lost none of his charisma, nor, despite being in his eighties, his patrician good looks. He wore an immaculate dark suit and a white silk scarf wound round his throat. At his side, his Japanese wife, years younger and many inches shorter, was dressed in an embroidered kimono and carried a fan. Her heavily made-up face and stiff, formal gestures made her look like a doll or perhaps an actor from the Kabuki theatre. With them was their daughter, closely resembling her mother, and two charmingly handsome men whom Eli recognised as his sons from his first marriage, all of whom shared in the aura of glamour.

As Eli gazed at the group the Count turned as though to make for the main doors. A banquet was being held in another part of the palace, where no doubt he was guest of honour. Eli would not be allowed entrance and had therefore only seconds to grab him or lose perhaps the only chance she'd ever get to speak to him. For now the paintings must wait. She pushed her way through the crowd towards the exit doors and took up position, just as he turned in her direction and his hangers-on regrouped themselves into a fan-shaped wake. She waited until he was a few yards from the doorway then stepped out into his path.

He stopped, startled, then his expression softened as he took in a pretty young woman.

'Excuse me, Count. I represent *Art Today*, a magazine based in London. We're huge admirers of your work.'

She was doing her best not to sound breathless.

'I am familiar with your journal. Indeed, its editor is an old friend of mine. One of the few critics in England whom I admire,' he replied in precise English.

His wife shifted impatiently at his side and Eli knew her time was short.

'I wanted to ask you... the atmosphere of your paintings is so thrilling but so disturbing. Did living in Berlin during such difficult times as the Great War contribute to their feeling of menace?'

She was aware he might dislike being reminded of such a troubled period, but it was a question she was certain had a bearing on the mysterious nature of his work.

His reply came quickly.

'I was only very briefly in Germany. Switzerland, where I continue to live, was my childhood home.'

'But I understood your family were stateless exiles, forced to return to Berlin from Paris in 1914. Rilke writes...'

He interrupted her. 'My family like many others at that time suffered because we were Polish, despite the fact that

17

my mother was a Poniatowski, related to the last king of Poland. Please excuse me, my dear, but we have a banquet to attend.'

His voice was icily polite.

Eli watched as his wife took his arm. The crowd opened then closed over their retreating figures, like the returning waters of the Red Sea. Humiliation was as nothing to her astonishment. What he'd said made no sense. Nowhere had she come across any reference to royal connections. There were even those who questioned whether he had a right to the title of Count. And if the grand lineage he claimed for himself was a fabrication, perhaps equally was his claim to having passed an affluent boyhood in Switzerland. His refusal to allow any biographical information about his life suddenly took on new meaning. Publicly he justified his embargo on personal information by claiming it to be irrelevant, even distracting, from a true understanding of his art. Now, it seemed, his real purpose might be somewhat different, though it was hard to see why such a distinguished painter should risk the humiliation of being unmasked as a fake.

That night in her hotel room she turned again to Rilke's letters, searching for references to the young Balthus. There were several addressed to him, full of praise for his precocious talent and encouragement not to lose heart under the difficult conditions of his life. One of those conditions must surely have been his mother's passion for a man who wasn't his father. Had that given rise to the jealousy and repressed violence depicted again and again in his remarkable paintings? Rilke wrote to Merline:

> *I the 'image hunter' go up into my mountains, wild, taciturn, losing myself. But you, my delicious valley, my heart's flute… you have the innate, imperturbable patience of the landscape and the flute and the holy chalice! Let us not be satisfied with recounting a fable of the heart; let us create its myth.*

What would a sensitive young boy be expected to make of such an affair, she wondered as she lay awake, book in hand, until finally she lost consciousness in the early hours of the morning.

Berlin, 1993
Eli

The meeting with Balthus fuelled her desire to look further into the history of the Klossowski family, especially during their Berlin years, and having delivered her review of the Poussin exhibition to her editor she decided to make another visit. It would also be a chance to see Gunter.

She phoned her parents to tell them she wouldn't be coming up for the weekend as planned. Her father asked if her decision had anything to do with her new German boyfriend, and wasn't fooled by her denial. She must have talked about him more than she'd realised. Their only son had gone to live in Hong Kong and married a Chinese wife, and now they were afraid of losing their daughter too. Her father joked wryly that his children had inherited his family's wanderlust. His own father had been born in Morocco, moved to Spain and later on to Germany, where he married and brought up two children in Berlin. Her father and his brother were raised as non-religious Jews, who considered themselves more German than Jewish, until the family was forced to leave Berlin shortly before the Second World War.

'By the way,' her father said. 'That nice young man you were at college with, Simon, he got in touch. He's part of a solicitor's practice now in Kidderminster. I told him next time you're up we'd ask him over.'

'Yes, Dad. Let's do that.'

She knew what he was after and wasn't fooled. It had never worked, especially not with Simon, whose name still evoked feelings of sadness and guilt.

In Berlin she declined Bill's offer of a room in his apartment, and booked herself into a small hotel in Schöneberg. It was within easy reach of Kreuzberg but not on Gunter's doorstep. When she called to tell him of her plan to return to Berlin he'd seemed pleased, but warned her that much of his time would be taken up with preparations for his film. She hoped he didn't feel pressured because she was returning so soon. She didn't know if he was in love with her, or even if the word was in his vocabulary. In fact she knew very little about him at all, except that once he'd been married but had separated some years ago and was now married to his work. It was possible he saw her as little more than a pleasant diversion when the occasion offered. And yet the way he was when they were alone together made her feel sure there was more to it than that.

Her hotel was an anonymous post-war building, but her room had a table next to the window where she could work. Gunter called the morning after her arrival and invited her to join him and his team for dinner.

'It's just a small local restaurant. We still haven't found a financial backer so at present I'm using up my savings just to keep the project afloat,' he said, speaking German.

'You're sure you want me there under the circumstances?'

'Of course! I'm looking forward to seeing you.'

When she arrived at the restaurant the team were already two thirds through a second bottle of wine. Whatever trouble the film was in didn't seem to be getting them down. Gunter greeted her affectionately and introduced her to the company. She did her best to appear friendly, though all she wanted was to be alone with him. He asked a couple of people to move along and gestured her to a space next to him.

In deference to Eli, the group attempted to speak English, until they grew animated and forgot. They spoke so fast and with many private allusions, so that after a while she gave up trying to follow and observed them instead. They were arguing about the current state of German cinema, without any of the self-deprecating irony Brits used to hold confrontation at bay. For a moment she feared they might come to blows, though they were neither drunk nor uncivilised enough for that. Gunter said little, but whenever he spoke everyone paused to listen. It was clear he was the focus of the group. In an attempt to appear part of things Eli drank more than usual, and by the end of the meal her cheeks ached from smiling and she was fighting to keep her eyes from closing.

Out on the pavement the chill air sobered her up.

'Hang on, and I'll give you a lift,' Gunter said.

Feeling the outsider she was, she watched as he bid the others goodbye with easy familiarity, and wondered sourly as she climbed into his car whatever made her think she could become part of his life. He drove her to the hotel and pulled up outside.

'D'you want me to come up?'

Her face burned under his gaze, and she feared she might burst into tears.

'Well, do you or don't you?'

'If you like.'

He cut the engine. 'I haven't time for games, Eli. Either you want me and there's something between us, or you don't.'

He said it gently, but his voice expressed an underlying weariness that made her lack of trust seem childish and petty. He'd invited her to join him at a difficult time for the film, and done his best to include her. If it hadn't worked, it wasn't his fault.

'I do.'

'Good.' He reached out to touch her hand. 'It's late. Shall we go up?'

They got out of the car.

Uncertainty melted in the heat of desire, as his touch sent bolts of electricity through her body. Afterwards he slept and she lay listening to the rise and fall of his breathing. Whatever the outcome, there was no going back. The thought both exhilarated and terrified her. Not until the first faint light of dawn did she finally fall into a deep, dreamless sleep.

She woke to find him already dressed and ready to leave.

'I made you coffee. Only instant, I'm afraid, from the hotel supply.'

He placed the cup on the night table as she pulled herself upright.

'Thanks.'

She ran her fingers through her tangled hair. Her mouth felt dry and frowsty and she was sure she looked a fright, but none of that mattered.

'What are you going to do today?' he said, as he sat down on the edge of the bed.

'Maybe I'll go for breakfast to Café Einstein. Try to decide how to start looking for the Klossowskis. If the rain keeps off, I may go for a walk in Tiergarten or visit a gallery.'

'I wish I could join you.'

He finished his coffee and stood up. 'I'll be through around seven. Would you like to come round to my place for supper?'

'Great! Eightish?'

He nodded, kissed her and was gone.

At the Einstein, the first sitting of professionals en route to the office was giving place to a more leisured crowd. She took down paper from the rack at the entrance, made her way to a free table and ordered breakfast with the special Viennese coffee the café was famous for. Next to her a couple were discussing a theatre production they'd seen by the avant-garde French director, Mnouchkine. For a while Eli tried to follow their conversation, but though her German was gradually improving she couldn't keep up. She'd begun to realise that what divided languages was not merely grammar and vocabulary. Each had its own personality, its own body language even, to which it forced the user to submit. Perhaps that was why Rilke had had to abandon his native German after the horrors of the Great War, and turned to what he perceived as the untainted clarity of French.

When she'd finished a copious breakfast of sausage, cheese, fruits and yoghurt, she looked over to the tall window on the far side of the café. A patch of blue sky looked big enough to make a sailor a goodly pair of trousers, so she paid her bill and set off for Tiergarten.

The park was full of young children and fathers who threw balls for them and ran behind their wobbly bikes, wiping away their tears whenever they toppled over. She tried to imagine Gunter as one of them. Bill had told her he'd had a son with his ex-wife, who must now be in his teens. He'd never mentioned him and she wondered if they were close. She recalled a photo on his desk of a lanky boy with hair down to his shoulders and slanting green eyes that might be him.

Clouds suddenly overwhelmed the blue and it came on to rain heavily. The fathers bundled their children into waterproofs and took their leave whilst Eli, less well prepared, ran for shelter. The nearest public building was the Akademie der Künste where they were advertising an exhibition called 'Berlin 1900'. With the rain giving no sign of letting up, she bought a ticket and went up to the first floor.

There were only a handful of visitors, several of whom looked old enough to have been alive when the photographs that lined the walls were taken. They peered intently at the unblemished streets and pompous grandeur of the pre-war city. One old woman wearing a dark costume and fox fur complete with head, had tears running down her wrinkled cheeks. No doubt she'd lived through the Weimar years of economic collapse and survived the devastation of the Second World War. It was impossible to imagine what she must be feeling.

Eli moved on to the second room, which was concerned with theatre. There were photographs of stage productions and portraits of famous people such as the Russian director Meyerhold and the Austrian Max Reinhardt, together with several well-known actors of the day. Then, just as she was about to enter the third room, she stopped in front of a painting. It was an almost life-size portrait of a woman, tall and voluptuous with strong features and dark flashing eyes like a gypsy. Her head was half-turned towards the viewer, lips slightly parted as if about to break into laughter, and her thick, unruly hair framed her face in a bob. Her dress, made of some light summery material, swirled about her as she moved her body as though to music, revealing from beneath the hem one neatly arched foot like a bird's. She was so alive it seemed as though at any minute she might step out from the frame. Eli leaned down to read the label below. It said, 'Baladine Dancing'!

With an excitement she could scarcely contain, she peered again at the label to make sure there was no mistake. Baladine was the name by which Balthus' mother was generally known, though Rilke called her Merline. Balthus' father, Erich Klossowski, had worked in the theatre with Max Reinhardt as a set designer, so it would be quite possible to find her in the company of the other exhibits. Eli had once seen a rather blurry photograph of her in a book about Rilke, standing stiffly at his side, as tall as he was yet somehow diminished by his presence. Here, before marriage or the turbulence of exile, she stood forth in all the exuberance of her girlish beauty.

She pulled her camera out of her pocket and glanced round to see if the guard was looking. The exhibition would close soon and the picture would no doubt disappear into whatever vault it had come from, perhaps never to be seen again. She must capture Merline in all her glory whilst she could.

Berlin, May 22nd 1921
Merline

I am feeble, feeble in everything, René. I have no place. I am a reed balanced in one hand or rather an uprooted thing which has no home anywhere and I no longer have any character. I am like someone one locks up in an empty room and who eternally bangs her head against the four walls. I am prepared like Esther for these months of summer without you. I do not know these places you speak to me about, René, but since you consider me like a sick person I will only see you as my guardian. No, no, no, no! You know that these many months I have wanted to see you and love you. I have wanted to live near you. It is the pain of using up my heart and soul on notepaper. I understand very well that the presence of your princely friend makes mine impossible. I hope that your meeting together proves useful for your future.

She folded up the paper and shoved it away in the desk drawer. She was empty and out of tears. If she were condemned to wait out her life in this terrible city, she would endure it with stoicism and without complaint. No more tearing at the walls with her bare hands until her fingers bled whilst dreaming of the paradise she had created for her lover in that other country, the same hands that had repaired and decorated his walls and turned his garden from a stony wilderness into a blossoming Eden. Spring would have already turned to summer in that gentler climate, and the roses she had planted for him would be in bloom. He would show them off to his princely benefactor and her name would scarcely be mentioned.

He was a genius but he was also a coward, who feared the demands of flesh and blood. He would love her as long as she remained an abstract, communicating only in words, passionate words full of gratitude and esteem. In Geneva she had endured the separations he demanded. But here, in the darkness of this hated city, bitterness and despair consumed her. She had given everything she had to create for him the haven he craved, and her reward was to be exiled from it.

London, 1993
Eli

As the Heathrow Express snaked into town, Eli gazed out at the rows of suburban houses with their neat pocket-sized gardens, uniform in the soft grey English light. After the pockmarked grandeur of Berlin, the landscape spoke to her only of paltriness. Sharpened by absence, she saw only the worst in these familiar surroundings and it was no comfort that custom would soon dull the senses and soften the anguish of separation until she forgot she'd ever been away.

For the first few days she moped about her flat in Chalk Farm, fighting the desire to call Gunter and doing her best to focus on the article about Balthus and the influence of his Berlin years that she wanted Michael, her editor, to commission. The discovery of Merline's portrait had whetted her determination to find out more about this woman who fascinated her yet remained a mystery evoked by the letters and the portrait that brought her so vividly to life. Rilke referred again and again to the work she sent him – paintings, drawings and pastels – but so far Eli could find no record of them. It seemed, as with so many female artists, she'd been written out of history.

She got the picture lab to make an enlargement of the snapshot she'd taken in the museum, and was struck by how much more earthy and robust Merline appeared than her son. Far from aristocratic there was something bucolic about her. Eli imagined a deep, infectious laugh, and a voice that went from caressing to shrill in a moment.

The absence of any response from Merline herself to Rilke's outpourings was increasingly frustrating. Despite help elicited from a librarian in the British Library who'd taken a shine to her, nothing had come to light. One day she mentioned her frustration to a colleague at the magazine.

'I know it sounds odd, but I feel I owe it her. To give her her place in the story.'

'Rilke's story, or Balthus'?'

'Both. It's because of her they knew each other. She's the lynchpin, an interesting character and an artist in her own right.'

'Have you tried the Senate House Library at London University? It's a cornucopia of oddities and weird bequests, mostly the collection of an old librarian who started work there soon after the Second World War and only retired a couple of years ago at a great age. People gave him stuff considered too trivial for other collectors. If you like I'll lend you my card.'

She thanked him and set out at once.

The library was on the first floor of the Senate House building and since the lift was out of order, she walked up the stairs. At the counter she slipped a hastily scribbled note with Merline's various aliases to the librarian.

As the woman disappeared into the cataloguing room, she went over to the window to calm her nerves. Looking out through the dusty foliage of the huge plane trees, tall as the terraces of once grand houses they half obscured, she thought how much she loved this part of London that still retained an echo of its intellectual heyday. In the early years of the century Beatrice and Sidney Webb had set up their pioneering idea of a new university and Bertrand Russell and Maynard Keynes had frequented the elegant drawing rooms of Virginia Woolf and that preposterous benefactor of the arts, Ottoline Morrell. How different from the Klossowskis, driven into stateless exile and forced to return to the chaos that was Germany. Was Merline grateful, she wondered, for Rilke's advice about visas and money that poured forth in letter after letter? Or were the hardships she endured too overwhelming to be assuaged by a mere letter?

The return of the librarian interrupted her thoughts. She returned to the desk and was handed a battered slim volume and a form to sign, agreeing to return the book within three weeks. Her mouth was dry with excitement as she read the faded gilt lettering on the worn leather cover, *Lettres de Mme Merline Klossowska au poète Rainer Maria Rilke, 1908–26*. Clutching the book to her bosom, she descended the staircase at a run.

Paris, 1907–14
Merline

The first time they met was in Paris; she was twenty-one and he thirty-two. She was aware men found her desirable with her dark eyes, slender figure and Slavic accent, but less confident of her ability to captivate a great poet such as Rilke. A mutual friend, a Swedish psychologist, brought him to her and Erich's apartment one evening for dinner. She was flattered that he'd agreed to come and took great pains in preparing a simple meal of fish and vegetables, being informed he was particular about what he ate.

She was struck at once by his courteous manner and strange, slightly glaucous blue gaze that looked at you as though you were the most intriguing thing in the world. They spoke German because Inge, the Swede, was more fluent in that language than French. She and Erich embarked on a lengthy dialogue concerning the symposium she'd just been attending. Rilke turned to Merline and remarked how in the normal course of things he preferred to speak French.

'In general, I feel more at home in French culture. I suspect you agree.'

'Indeed! The German language is so ready to shape one's thoughts.'

He smiled his agreement. But before the conversation could develop further, Inge's voice interrupted them as she vigorously defended her latest theory against Erich's equivocations. Rilke joined in and Merline did her best to pretend interest in an argument she found largely tedious. As she observed the three of them together, she thought how if she and Rilke were alone he would reveal an altogether different persona from the one he displayed at present.

She got up, removed the empty plates from the table and, aided by Inge, brought in fresh dishes for dessert. Rilke and Erich fell to discussing Daumier, about whom Erich was writing a book. As they returned to their places, Rilke turned his attention back to the women and, with only a passing glance at Merline, asked Inge about the book she was preparing to publish. Needing little encouragement, she launched into a detailed description of the theory of child development she was working on whilst Merline, as she struggled to keep her eyes open, thought how her actual child would shortly wake, demanding to be fed.

'I wish such illuminating ideas had been around during my own childhood,' she heard Rilke say. 'They might have prevented some of the bigotry that caused me so much misery!'

Erich intervened. 'All those pretty puttos and innocent beggar boys, as they're depicted in paintings! It's as if only idealised perfections of innocence are to be tolerated in art, rarely the fractious realities of childhood.'

'If children are fractious it's because they're frustrated,' Merline cut in sharply. 'And who can blame them? I, for one, couldn't wait to become adult.'

'That is true. We should allow children more license to be themselves,' Rilke responded.

'Precisely!' Inge agreed.

Erich remained silent.

Later that night when their guests had left and she had washed and put away the dishes, she lay in bed beside her sleeping husband, reliving the events of the evening. She felt restless and didn't fall asleep for a long time. It was only a couple of hours later when the dawn light seeped in through the blinds that she was woken by the child, and for the rest of the day she felt troubled and unsettled, which she put down to lack of sleep.

A few days later she and Erich received an invitation to visit Rilke at his apartment. She was deeply flattered, especially as it suggested the supper at their apartment hadn't been a complete failure. She dressed carefully and since the weather was fine, they decided to walk rather than take the tram.

He greeted them both warmly, though to Merline's chagrin she could detect nothing special in his manner towards her. Erich asked him about his work, saying he would love to hear him read something. Rilke went over to his lectern and began to recite from his latest volume, *Le Livre d'heures*. She found it hard to focus on the meaning of the words, but their rhythm and the musical cadence of his voice were intensely moving. Afterwards she was still too emotional to take much part in the conversation and then it was time to leave. He shook both their hands, retaining hers a moment longer and holding her gaze before bidding them both goodbye.

Early the following week he sent a note to tell them he was leaving Paris. Merline knew she had no right to feel disappointment, yet she was bereft. As she pushed the baby's pram along familiar streets, it was hard not to feel the banality of her existence. When she closed her eyes she could still see the milky blue of his intense gaze and hear his voice chanting the mesmerising lines of his verse.

Their next meeting took place a few years later, though she'd forgotten nothing of their previous encounter. She was on her way one fine day in early summer to visit her sister, when suddenly there he was, walking towards her along the Boulevard Raspail. He greeted her with a warm smile, remarking on the extraordinary coincidence of their encounter that seemed to delight him as much as it did her. She recalled aloud the time in his apartment that she'd never forget, when he'd read from his latest book of poems to her and Erich.

'I can't tell you what that meant to me! You probably don't even remember.'

It was as much as she could do to stop herself from reaching out to seize his hand.

'I'm proud and touched to hear you say so. Especially since you're an artist yourself. Tell me, what have you been painting since we last met?'

The question embarrassed her. She could scarcely tell him that all she'd managed were a few scrappy drawings.

'Very little, I'm afraid... But I've given birth to another ravishing young son. That's the extent of my creativity!'

'Then I look forward to meeting him, together with the rest of your delightful family.'

If she had disappointed him he didn't show it.

'Perhaps you could come to tea tomorrow? I know Erich would be delighted to see you. We're living in St-Germain now.'

'I should like nothing better.'

'About four o'clock then?'

The clouds lifted and joy filled her heart as he took her hand and kissed it.

'Until tomorrow.'

The following afternoon she waited, the table laid with a lace cloth and her best china and some pastries nicely arranged on a pretty plate. The children had been fed so they'd be in a good mood and dressed in their nicest clothes and Erich had looked out a copy of his latest article to hand to Rilke on arrival. But he never came. Somehow she'd known he wouldn't. Domestic life held few enough charms for her husband let alone a great artist like him, who'd made it clear that dedication to his art required freedom from all trivia of ordinary existence.

The next day he sent a note, explaining his regret at having to leave Paris again in a hurry. He looked forward, he said, to meeting all the family as soon as he returned, including her two young boys. Gratified as she was, it was small compensation for the thought that they might never meet again. It only showed how foolish she'd been to build a casual acquaintance into something it could never be. It was time to banish daydreams and concentrate on being a better wife and mother, not to mention a better painter too.

A couple of months later war was declared. Merline and her family, like all the others living in Paris and holding German passports, were required to leave France on the next available train. Rilke would no doubt have been with them, had he remained.

Berlin, 1914–17
Merline

Although it was autumn when they arrived, Berlin felt shockingly cold and grey. At night she dreamed of Paris, shining like a bright mirage through the fog that embraced this chaotic city with its grim streets and ugly people, its marching soldiers and armoured vehicles that roared up and down the boulevards day and night.

She had left behind all inessential belongings in her studio at 15, Rue Malebranche as hostage to the time when they would return. Whatever her previous frustrations the life they'd lived there seemed now like a lost idyll, full of art and literature and friends destined for great things. Here existence was reduced to its most sordid and people preoccupied only with foraging enough food for the next meal. The cries of quarrelling neighbours, caught like rats in the trap that was their overcrowded tenement, reverberated up the staircase and through the walls.

They were staying with her brother and his wife and child in a flat barely sufficient for its three existing inhabitants. Merline liked her brother, a fellow painter, though they weren't close having seen little of each other over past years. He was cheerful and easy-going. Her sister-in-law, on the other hand, was highly strung and fretted over the least thing, including the stress of having four more people in her already crowded flat. Merline did her best to help out, but it was impossible to prevent the children from getting under everyone's feet and adding to the tension.

Erich, never naturally sociable, absented himself at every opportunity. In general the move to Germany was proving easier for him and he felt relatively at home in Berlin. His main problem was the lack of domestic order and his temper, short at the best of times, was constantly tried by the children's rowdy chaos and what he considered Merline's overindulgence.

In early November it snowed but quickly melted, leaving behind piles of gritty slush under a relentlessly grey sky. Even at midday it never seemed to get light. Merline bundled the children into their coats and sent them down to the courtyard to let off steam. But minutes later they were back again, complaining the place was dark and dirty and the people rude and unfriendly. Balthus had been collecting the remnants of snow from a windowsill to play snowballs, when an elderly resident ordered the boys to stop at once and to go back indoors. The humiliation of being spoken to so harshly hurt the children's sensitive pride and henceforth they refused to play outside, despite Erich's exasperated orders to stand up for themselves.

To keep them occupied Merline sometimes joined in their games, chasing through the apartment during hide-and-seek in search of whoever was hidden inside a cupboard or under a bed, then hauling them out with shrieks of delighted merriment. Erich exploded.

'You're worse than your children! You turn this cattle pen into a madhouse.'

'D'you think you're the only one to suffer from the conditions we live in, without room for work or play?' she retorted.

But he wasn't listening.

Once she burst out, 'Does it ever occur to you your constant complaining is harder to endure than your children's behaviour?'

But mostly she kept quiet.

The tension was relieved when Erich got a job as stage designer with Max Reinhardt's theatre company, with the prospect that now he could find them a place of their own and no longer be beholden to her brother's charity.

But for Merline the move proved to be an exchange of one set of problems for another. Working with lively, creative people during the day and often late into the evening improved Erich's spirits, and with the income it provided if she was careful she could buy the family what they needed. But they had only one decent sized room in which they lived, ate, and the two adults also slept, whilst the children occupied the other. Worst of all there was once again nowhere for Erich to work.

'Can't you at least tidy the place up when the boys go to bed? You've got all day to make as much mess as you like!' he grumbled as he gathered up the toys he'd stumbled over on his return from the theatre.

What really infuriated him was when she and the children made free with his art materials for their own use.

'How am I supposed to work when you help yourselves to my pens and paper whenever you please for your own scribblings!'

She swallowed her anger and refrained from retorting that lack of space and time made painting or even drawing well-nigh impossible for her. She'd become little more than a domestic drudge, no different from the neighbours she tried unsuccessfully to befriend and who preferred spying on one another to exchanging a few words to add a little colour to the day. The odious smells of their cooking, cabbage and meat boiled for hours to render it edible, filled the house, seeping up the staircase into every apartment. Convivial evenings full of talk and laughter she'd known in Paris were a distant memory in this place where life was a daily struggle to stay alive and where, even if they'd had friends, she'd have been too exhausted to enjoy their company.

As spring came, the weather improved. Desperate to get outside into the fresh air, Merline packed up a picnic and she and the children took the trolley-bus out to one of the lakes. They walked through woods where leaves were at last bursting into life, and when they reached the edges of the still icy water the sun came out from behind the clouds. The air felt warm, though the wind was chill, and they breathed in scents of earth and foliage. After the cramped, stuffy apartment the boys ran like two dogs let off the lead, whooping and leaping with unrestrained joy. Merline ran too, arms outstretched and shouting aloud for the fun of it.

With the days growing longer and grey skies giving way to patches of brilliant blue, she was seized anew by the need to draw, using every free moment to make hasty sketches on whatever scrap of paper she'd managed to steal from Erich's precious store. It wasn't serious work but it gave her pleasure, reminding her she wasn't just a domestic drudge.

Working hard at the theatre, Erich spent less and less time with the family, and often when he returned at night he stayed up making drawings and calculations for some new production long after Merline was in bed and asleep. At times she asked herself what, if anything, gave purpose to her life. Not her marriage, which offered neither of them the pleasure or satisfaction they'd once hoped for. What love she had left was for her children, and her belief in them was what nourished her. They were both exceptionally gifted, Pierre with his father's ordered intelligence and meticulous attention to whatever task he undertook, whether writing about Greek drama in his school book or rewiring the table lamp that kept fusing in the living room. Balthus had no interest in practical things but could draw like an angel and both boys were miles ahead of their peers at school, which was another reason for their hating it.

Balthus, especially, suffered constant torment from his classmates, who ridiculed his Parisian accent and French clothes, even though they were as patched and darned as their own. Though small and wiry, he soon learned to defend himself. Flying into a rage and grabbing hold of his tormentor, he head-butted him in the chest or belly heedless of punishment and forced him to the ground. This earned him the respect of fellow pupils, and eventually the teasing abated. But the masters continued to pick on him, mistaking his precocious intelligence for arrogance and his shyness for insolence.

Merline requested a meeting at the school to explain that her sons were finding the transition from the French to the German education system difficult. The headmaster saw her request as criticism of the school and an attempt to raise her sons above the rest, which only increased the hostility. She was horrified by what she saw as the unimaginative rigidity of the masters, and she explained to the boys that their own enthusiasm for knowledge was the chief cause of the teachers' anger because it pointed out their own lack of intellectual curiosity. At home Balthus took his revenge by mocking his tyrants, and his impersonations made Merline laugh until she forgot the injustices that lay behind them. If it hadn't been for those children she could scarcely have endured another day in this city.

Erich took little part in their daily lives, either at home or at school, leaving such matters to her. When first she and he had met, his scholarship and love of argument had impressed her, and his erudition made her ashamed of her own ignorance and laziness. As her intellectual superior he'd presented her with a goal to aspire to, but the more she learned, the more she found his opinions pedantic. Even his personal habits, such as the methodical way he laid out his papers or arranged his clothes on the chair at night, irritated her. She had constantly to circumvent his outbursts of anger whenever the expected routine was disrupted, and anticipating his moods exhausted her so that at times she felt as though she were drowning.

She was aware her own moodiness didn't help the situation. The spontaneity that in youth had been one of her charms for him, he now found wearisome, even vulgar.

'Do you imagine it's easy living with a woman who's even more childish than her own sons?' he demanded during one of their clashes.

He spoke in anger, but his words wounded her as they were meant to.

One night she was standing naked at the unshuttered window contemplating the glory of the full moon, when he ordered her peremptorily to cover herself.

'D'you want the neighbours to see you flaunting yourself like that?'

It was as if he had slapped her. She turned to face him in all her challenging nakedness.

'And what if I do?'

'You're not a young girl any more. Perhaps you'd do well to remember that!'

Despite her rage, her hands went up to cover her breasts in an automatic gesture of shame. The nakedness he'd once found beautiful, the cause of desire, was now merely embarrassing. She vowed never to appear naked before him again. But the anger settled deep and refused to be subdued. She would not let him extinguish that spontaneity that gave her life and was the expression of all that made it worth living.

From that day on she detached herself more and more from Erich, and as a result things became easier between them. There were still arguments and what made them harder to bear was that the children heard every word through the thin walls of the apartment. Sometimes as she lay in bed at night going over the events of the day, feelings of resentment drove her to get up and find refuge with one of the boys for the remainder of the night. In the morning Erich never mentioned her absenting herself, but his silence added to the store of ill-feeling.

In an attempt to recover some common ground she did her best to find friends amongst his colleagues at the theatre, where he spent more and more of his time. But they too seemed to have caught the fever of nationalism that had possessed the nation. She knew, of course, this was not confined to Germany. In France it was what had driven out her family as soon as war was declared. But the bigotry and fanaticism that each day she heard declaimed ever more stridently in the

44

streets and newspapers was becoming increasingly alarming, with communists and nationalists denouncing each other with equal bitterness in the face of this interminable war. If she still dreamed of Paris as a lost paradise, in her heart she feared that when it was over even there things would not return to what they had been. The world would be changed, and how would people like herself without papers or clear national identity be allowed to return to France?

London, 1994
Eli

Eli completed an outline for her article on the influence of Balthus' Berlin years on his early work, and submitted it to her editor. She left out most of the personal data gleaned from Rilke's letters, knowing that fear of ostracism by the art world or, worse still, costly lawsuits, would make Michael reject it. She focused instead on the political and cultural atmosphere of the period. A German journal she'd approached in Berlin also expressed interest. Balthus, it seemed, was big in Germany right now, following a successful exhibition in New York.

'If I can't say what I want in his lifetime, I'll wait. He's an old man. He can't live forever!' she told Michael.

He sighed. 'I admire your tenacity. Unlike me, you're young. You can afford to wait. Meanwhile, go to Berlin and write me something about 'Die Neue Wilden'. They've a show coming up and there's a lot of interest over here.'

Permission Eli had sought to research in the library of the old Tate Gallery came through unexpectedly, and she decided to put off her departure for a few days. The archives were housed in a low-ceilinged attic room above the main entrance, overlooking the murky waters of the Thames. On windy days it felt like being in the rigging of a ship, and she loved it. She intended to look through the library's collection of catalogues of past exhibitions for interviews Balthus might have given or articles written about him by people less discreet than current critics.

On the second day she turned up a catalogue for an exhibition at MOMA in New York in 1984, and found what she had been looking for. It was a lengthy introduction written by the curator, Sabine Rewald, and filed with it an article also written by Rewald for the *New York Times*, together with some correspondence and notes of conversations recorded with the artist. As she read through the papers she realised why she hadn't come across any of this material before. Rewald wrote that Balthus' grandfather on his mother's side, far from having Polish royal connections as Balthus had claimed, was a Jewish cantor from Pest. She picked out a letter at random. It was from Balthus in response to Rewald's essay, accusing her of spreading malicious lies, and casting aspersions on her reputation as a scholar.

'I am not Jewish,' he wrote. 'But denying it becomes

disagreeable. I have many Jewish friends – Yehudi Menuhin, for instance, who is one of the greatest men of our time and a good neighbour, and I have no wish to be misinterpreted.'

She leafed through the rest of the correspondence. The dispute, far from being resolved, had become increasingly bitter. Rewald refused to recant and Balthus broke off all relations. One thing was clear. If Rewald's claims were true, the persona Balthus presented to the world was an invention.

Intrigued, she tried to think of reasons he might have had for denying his roots. The family's life in Germany after the Great War would undoubtedly have been made more difficult by the fact of being Jewish, and Rilke, his beloved mentor, had expressed anti-Jewish sentiments in some of his letters and played down his own Jewish blood. Perhaps Balthus, flattered and encouraged throughout his childhood for his exceptional talents, had felt it necessary to invent a history equal to his distinction. She had seen for herself how he delighted in impersonating the grand prince and, like the cunning cats in his paintings, enjoyed playing the trickster to a credulous public. Salvador Dali had also created a mask to protect and amuse himself, until self-parody took over and he paid for it with his art. And Balthus' later paintings, in Eli's view, had similarly lost their fire – 'The Painter and his Model', for instance, where a young girl, unreal as a puppet, kneels in frozen anticipation of her master's attention as he gazes absently out of the window. How had Merline reacted, she wondered, to the rewriting of their family history? Had she gone along with it or merely agreed to remain silent?

With so many unanswered questions, she decided to take a short break and make the long overdue visit to her parents. It was her young cousin's bat mitzvah, and though her parents had no truck with religion, they'd decided to make an exception for the sake of her father's only brother and accept the invitation. It would make all the difference, they said, if she accompanied them.

Returning home was always an emotional experience. The house where she and her brother had been brought up was shared during her early childhood with her paternal grandparents. Set in a large, rambling garden it provided the theatre for their games where, hidden after dark in the tree house their father had built, they told each other ghost stories until the wind suddenly blew out the candle and snatched away their half-empty pack of Smarties as if by alien hand. Then they scrambled down and ran for safety to the house and the supper their grandmother had waiting for them. Their grandfather often joined in their games, pretending to be a cowboy and herding the angry hens with a skipping rope until their mother, roused by the furious cackling, shouted at them to stop tormenting the poor creatures.

As they grew older they roamed further afield, into the bluebell wood and a stream where they caught minnows and the occasional stickleback they brought home in jam jars.

No one fussed as long as they were back by dark, though the fish never survived more than a day or two despite their best efforts.

Their little paradise came to an end when suddenly their grandfather died of a stroke, and shortly after their grandmother succumbed to Alzheimer's and had to be sent to a home. No longer did the enticing smells of her cooking greet them at suppertime or the wheezy cackle of his laughter lift their spirits after the long school day. A silent melancholy overtook the house, and when her parents were unable to afford the fees of the old people's home, a large chunk of the garden had to be sold off. The cedar was felled and where the rose garden and shrubbery had been a new estate sprang up, spreading like a rash until it swallowed up the neighbouring farm where they'd raised horses. A road was carved through the bluebell wood and when the time came to leave for university they did so easily, eager to leave behind a place that existed now in memory only.

It was a fine spring morning when she drove out of London and onto the M40 in her clapped-out Fiat Punto. In the city the green fingers of the horse chestnuts were starting to unfurl but in the countryside they were merely sticky brown buds. Leaving the motorway she wound down the window, breathing in air full of the scents of hawthorn blossom and newly-mown grass, and, turning up the radio, broke into song.

Her mother was waiting on the doorstep as she drove

into her parents' driveway as if sensing the moment of her daughter's arrival, and arms entwined they walked to the house. Her father emerged to greet her.

'You're looking peaky, my girl. Too many late nights!'

'No, Dad. Working hard.'

'Same thing. You're young. You need to get out and enjoy yourself.'

'That's why I'm here! Where am I sleeping?'

'Your old room,' her mother said. 'We're thinking of letting it to a student, but thought we'd better ask you first. While you're here perhaps you can see what can be thrown out and what you want to keep.'

A stab of childish resentment at the prospect of being usurped by a stranger made her retort, 'Maybe next time. I have to be back in London tomorrow night.'

The bat mitzvah was due to begin in an hour, so she went straight up to change. The reform synagogue was one she'd attended during a brief, rebellious flirtation with her father's faith. The service went on for hours, one incantation after another. Halfway through her father slipped out. She wanted to go too but feared it would be noticed. When the ceremony was finally over, they all trooped out and got into their cars. A lavish reception was being held at a nearby country club.

They arrived at a grand house that had once been a stately home, with a lake and extensive grounds. The reception was held in the ballroom, which had French windows that gave onto the garden. Guests sat at long tables, decorated with yellow jonquils and blue irises. Eli found herself seated between cousins of her own age, neither of whom she'd seen in years and scarcely recognised. Now and then, between courses, people came over to greet her, mainly girls she'd grown up with, married now and pregnant for the second or third time. She sensed a whiff of pity for her single state, and imagined them discussing her afterwards with their husbands. 'By all appearances she's not sacrificed the joys of family life for success. Look at the car she drives!'

A band struck up for dancing. She made an excuse to leave the table and took refuge on the far side of the dance floor near the open French windows. She'd known she'd be a fish out of water but not how humiliating the whole experience would be. She heard someone come up behind her and turned around. He held a glass of champagne in each hand and, as he handed her one, she recognised the man who'd married her best friend from primary school. She'd been invited to their wedding but hadn't been able to make it.

'I hear you've become a bit of a writer,' he said.

'Thanks.' She sipped the champagne. 'I'm not really a writer. I do the odd piece for an art review in London.'

'So what are you writing now?'

She took another sip. It was not a conversation she wished to pursue.

'Something on the painter Balthus.'

She assumed he wouldn't have heard of him and that'd be the end of it.

'That fellow who painted pictures of dreamy girls with their skirts pulled up over their fannies? I picked up a book of his stuff in a secondhand shop in Bristol when I was there on business. Evie made me put it away because of the kids.'

'I'm amazed you've even heard of him!' It came out before she could stop herself, and she saw him flinch.

'No doubt a sophisticated metropolitan like yourself makes no distinction between art and pornography. When you've got kids you can't afford to be quite so liberal.'

'How are Evie and the children?' she said, effusively friendly. 'We must get together next time I'm here. I'd love to have a proper catch-up.'

'I'll tell her.'

He smiled politely and turned on his heels.

'Give her my love!' she called to his retreating back.

He gave a brief wave of his hand and kept on walking.

'You stupid bitch!' she muttered furiously to herself. Downing her champagne, she left the ballroom via the door to the entrance hall.

There was a phone kiosk in one corner and she was seized by an impulse to talk to Gunter. She gave the number to the girl at the desk, who told her to go to the kiosk and wait to be put through. After a short delay she heard the foreign dial tone then the answerphone kicked in and Gunter's voice told her in German to leave a message. She hesitated then spoke hurriedly into the receiver.

'Hi Gunter, it's me, Eli. I'm at this dreadful family do, missing you. How's the film going? Call me when you get a minute.'

She gave him her parents' number and rang off, feeling worse than ever. The disembodied sound of his voice only increased her sense of separation. He wouldn't call back, even if he got the message.

She went out through the glass doors at the end of the hall and descended a flight of steps into the garden. Her only thought was to get as far away from the party as possible. She walked across the damp lawn to the edge of the lake and stood there watching the ducklings. Tiny balls of fluff made reckless dashes across the surface of the water before being rounded up by an anxious parent.

She was aware of someone coming up behind her, and a voice said, 'Pretty, though I wouldn't fancy their chances. Someone dumped a couple of terrapins in the lake last autumn.'

She turned round to see a slightly plump young man with a rosy face and cherubic smile.

'Simon! I didn't know you were here.'

She flung her arms around him, almost squashing the breath out of his body. It was several years since they'd last met. She searched his face for any residue of resentment, but saw only warmth. They'd attended sixth form college together and gone on to university, where they'd become lovers. Aged twenty and about to enter the second year of her course, she'd fallen pregnant. Simon had been thrilled, full of enthusiastic plans for sharing childcare throughout their final year and making a life together. But for Eli it was a catastrophe. Her parents would be devastated and she herself was utterly unprepared for motherhood or domestic life before she'd even tasted freedom. Without telling him, she went ahead with an abortion, knowing it would be harder to withstand the pressure he'd put on her to keep the child. It was her future, she told herself, and she alone must make the decision.

Whatever sense of loss she'd experienced was nothing compared to Simon's. He was heartbroken, his dream shattered. The kindest thing, she'd decided, was a clean break and they spent a miserable final year doing their best to avoid each other. Later when they left university and she moved to London she wrote him a letter, apologising for the pain she'd caused and doing her best to reassure him that though she didn't regret her action, nothing that had happened between them was his fault.

He replied briefly, saying he harboured no bitterness but found it impossible to get the image of the child they might have had together out of his mind. It was a beautiful letter, simple and sincere, and she wept the tears she'd never shed, before pushing the whole thing as far as possible out of her mind. All that was a long time ago, and now here he was.

'Wow!' he said. 'I'd forgotten what strength you've got for a small woman.'

He pulled down his jacket, which had ridden up over his rather broad hips and straightened his clip-on bow tie.

'I'm so glad to see you! I was feeling like a fish out of water, and then you turn up!'

'A fellow fish! I come up alternate weekends to take turns with my sister. Dad had a stroke.'

'I'm so sorry… You always were such a good son.'

He shrugged. 'Mother never enjoyed the duties of carer and now fate's condemned her to it! Sod's law, I guess!'

'I remember her as quite a career woman.'

'Recently she got a job with a cancer counselling trust, which has improved things a bit. It means someone else has to look after Dad on Saturdays.'

'Still, you're looking good on it.'

'Well fed, you mean! Domestic life!'

'You're married!'

'No such luck, I'm afraid. We split up in the New Year. I'm moving next month to a new practice in London.'

'Why didn't you tell me? I'm good at being a shoulder to cry on.'

He laughed. 'Dear Eli! Actually it was me who broke it off this time.'

She blushed, embarrassed by her assumption that he was always the one to get dumped. She'd forgotten how intuitive he was.

'Dad said you'd started a practice here. He got it wrong, as usual.'

'I was going to, with Melanie, my ex-girlfriend. When we split up I decided this was the moment to make a move.' He gazed at her. 'And you? I heard you were in Berlin.'

'On and off. Mainly London. I write for *Art Today*.'

'I always said you'd do well.'

'According to most of the people here, I'm a lost cause!'

'Screw them! Their only measure of success is six children and a salary in six figures.'

They linked arms as they continued their walk around the lake. It was strange how familiar it felt after all this time.

'So you'll be selling that house you bought with the legacy from your grandmother? My parents still hold you up as a shining example of what youth should be.'

'I doubt it'll buy much in London.'

'Still, I admire you!'

'For what? You never wanted to settle down!'

'That's true. But at least you know what matters in life.'

'And you don't? You're less easily satisfied, that's all.'

They were silent for a moment.

'Are you with anyone?'

'No one in particular.'

Suddenly she found herself fighting tears. All these couples with their successful lives, whereas she...

'Shit! You always do this to me!'

'Do what?'

'See through to the messed up fraud I am!'

'Seriously, what's going on?'

She sighed. 'I guess I'm in love with a man who doesn't know whether or not he loves me.'

'Why doesn't he?'

'Oh... he's got better things to think about! Besides he's

years older and married to his career. Anyway, I'm not prepared to sacrifice my life and go and live in a foreign country where I can't even speak the language properly.'

'So you don't love him.'

She laughed despite herself.

'Your problem is you never want what's on offer. So follow your star!'

'That takes courage.'

'Not something I've noticed you lack.'

'I wish that were true.'

They resumed their walk.

'So what else are you up to?'

'Work wise?'

She told him of the piece she was trying to write about Balthus, how he'd reinvented himself and in the process condemned his mother, a painter herself, to silence.

'Sounds like it should be a novel!' Simon said.

'Maybe, only I wouldn't be the one to write it.'

'Why not?'

'Well… I'm not that kind of writer.'

They were halfway across the lawn, and from the open windows of the ballroom a klezmer band struck up.

'Hear that?' she cried, suddenly joyful. 'It always makes me want to dance!'

He reached out and seized her by both hands.

Geneva, 1919
Merline

The war was finally over, and in the spring of 1919 Merline received an answer to her prayers. Friends of her brother offered to find somewhere for her and the boys to stay for a couple of months in Switzerland, if she could find means to get them there. Pierre was fourteen and Balthus eleven and they were as eager as she was to leave Berlin. But first the problem of visas had to be overcome and, equally problematic, Erich must be persuaded to let them go.

Merline knew that once she got to Switzerland she would do her best never to return to Germany, whereas Erich had found a niche for himself in Munich working at the theatre with Max Reinhardt. She and the children had remained in Berlin so most of the time they were living apart. She told herself that he would scarcely miss her and it would be as easy for him to visit the boys in Switzerland as to travel to Berlin. But she knew things would not be that simple.

In the end he agreed to the boys accompanying her for a holiday, though all the way to the border she worried he might change his mind and be waiting for them. Not until they'd crossed over did she breathe more easily and feel something of her old courage returning. As she gazed out at the passing landscape with its orchards and vineyards and pretty villages scattered across rolling hills, she thought they might almost be in France.

For the first couple of weeks they were to stay in Berne with her brother's friends, whilst waiting for the apartment they were renting in Geneva to come free. It was remarkable how quickly she became used to having space to herself after the cramped conditions of Berlin, the luxury of a bed of her own and in the morning sitting on the balcony drinking coffee and breathing in the clean air that came down from the mountains. Later she wandered through the local market, surveying a forgotten array of vegetables and cheeses and choosing whatever was needed for the convivial meals they shared – simple pleasures she'd almost forgotten.

Two weeks passed in a trice, and when finally she and the boys arrived in Geneva they found the whole town bathed in light reflected from the lake. It cast a surreal brightness over the streets and squares, melting away the last of winter gloom. This, she felt, was somewhere she could stay for the rest of her life.

The apartment they were renting was in the Rue du Pré-Jérôme, modest for three people but after Berlin it felt like a palace. It was on the third floor, with windows on two sides and no tall buildings with grim courtyards to obscure the view of trees and sky. Each day as she walked the boys to school, she lifted her face to the sun and counted her blessings. If her visa came through, they would be able to stay for the rest of the year.

As soon as they moved in she started repainting the rooms, pale colours to maximise the light she craved. When she had finished, she hung up the boys' drawings and some of her own watercolours and set out jugs of flowers and grasses they had gathered during their walks by the lake on every windowsill. Early morning birdsong from the open windows was louder than the distant rumble of trams and cars, and the memory of their former life was fading fast. The cost of everything in comparison to Berlin was, however, shocking and made her meagre funds less sufficient than ever. But even this was not enough to quell the feeling of joy in just being alive with which she awoke each day.

A couple of weeks after their arrival, she received a small package with a note from Rilke. He had heard from her friends in Berne that she and her sons were now in Geneva and asked if he might call on them the following afternoon. She read the note again in a state of agitation. There would be just herself and the boys, no one else present to divert or engage him in conversation.

He'd dropped in unexpectedly at her friends' apartment just as she was leaving Berne, and her pleasure at seeing him again after so many years had filled her with uncharacteristic shyness. Amid the talk and the coming and going they'd scarcely managed to exchange more than a few words, and neither of them referred to the war or Berlin. Their conversation had been about Paris, as if mutual longing to return there was the single thing that connected them. Delighted as she was by the encounter, she had determined to make nothing of it and to see it as an accidental occurrence that would not be repeated.

In the package was a book of sonnets by a young French

poetess. It shamed her to think how he considered her to be so much more of a reader than she was. She hadn't commented that time when he'd read to her and Erich in Paris, because she knew herself unqualified to give judgement. Yet whenever they met he asked her about her painting, as though talking to a fellow artist. She'd determined to live up to his expectations, but too many things had intervened and time had passed.

She wrote a note to thank him for his gift and to say how she and the boys looked forward to his visit the following day. That afternoon, whilst the children were still at school, she ran to the bakery at the end of the street to buy a fruit tart and some of the boys' favourite almond biscuits. She had some China tea left, which she remembered he liked, and laid the table with her prettiest cups. At the centre she placed a bunch of white narcissi whose delicate scent filled the room, and sat down to wait.

He arrived before the children. She heard his footstep on the stair and made herself wait for the bell before jumping to her feet and running to the door. He stood there, handsome in his tweed suit and high starched collar, holding out a bunch of yellow cowslips. She buried her face in them and, with a delight she made no attempt to hide, invited him in.

He looked around him at the pretty room.

'You've made it beautiful!'

'Yes! The afternoon light here is always lovely. It faces west.'

He wandered round, examining the drawings and watercolours one by one that hung on the walls.

'Are these yours?'

'That one's mine. Most of them the boys did. They're so talented.'

He peered more closely at her watercolour.

'You make me feel everything you paint! Look here, how the petals are just ready to drop. I can feel their heavy velvetiness.'

'Please go on! Like the cat, I can take any amount of stroking.'

He turned to her. With her wide, slightly slanting eyes and high cheekbones she resembled a cat. Her body, too, had the sensual grace of a sleek animal.

'The boys have inherited your talent.'

She blushed. 'Do you mind waiting for tea till they get home? I promised them we would. They're so excited at the prospect of meeting you again.'

He asked her what she was currently working on and she told him she had been able to achieve little since Paris, where most of these paintings had been done. He made her describe where and when each one had been carried out and soon it was as if they were back there once more and life was rich with possibility. They spoke in French, even though German was for both their native tongue, and he told her how for him the clear light from the Alps as it danced over the lake brought a breath of France to the streets and squares of the old town. Soon, however, he would have to return to Germany. He'd been putting it off now for almost a month.

They heard footsteps bounding up the stairs two at a time and the boys burst into the apartment. They threw down their schoolbags and rushed forward to greet their visitor with an eagerness that reminded him, he said, of their mother. Pierre at fourteen was more reserved but Balthus was full of chatter and laughter.

'What d'you think of the exhibition of Chinese water-colours that's just opened in town?' he demanded eagerly, even before taking off his coat.

'I confess I haven't seen it yet. But I shall make a point of doing so at the first opportunity,' Rilke replied.

He found the boy's precocious enthusiasm very engaging. There was something unusually enchanting about the whole family.

The following day Merline received a note, thanking her for a delightful afternoon and asking whether the three of them would care to join him for a picnic that coming Sunday if the weather was fine. He signed himself 'René'.

The day was beautiful so they took the tram to the edge of the city and walked along the rim of the lake. Despite the clear sky and only a scud of clouds, the wind from the mountains still carried a chill, reminding them the snows up there had not yet melted. René had brought a basket containing sausage, cheese, tomatoes, fresh rolls, a bottle of French wine and even a rug to sit on.

They ate their picnic next to the water, and as the sun grew warmer the boys ran off to play. Merline lay back against the bank, her eyes closed in utter contentment. She felt poised on the edge of some great adventure that had been lying in wait for her even before she left Paris. For so long her appetite for life had been starved, until existence seemed to have lost all savour and she had scarcely energy to carry out routine tasks for the sake of the children. Now it was returning, and as the darkness retreated the long period of anguish was drawing to a close.

But with this feeling came the consciousness that she was living in a dead relationship. It was neither Erich's fault nor hers but an incompatibility that had become ever more apparent over the years. On her side the effect was to negate all that was creative and joyful within her, whilst Erich found himself exasperated by a woman who showed little enthusiasm for the things that mattered to him and shared few of his values. The thought of living together again was intolerable.

'Your sons are a credit to you. And to Erich, of course,' René said, breaking into her thought.

'You like children?'

'I like yours. I have a daughter but I rarely see her.'

'Does that make you sad?'

'Sometimes it does. Mostly I think we are better apart.'

'Is there a parent who isn't torn between love for their children and the desire to live without encumbrance? Sometimes I long to be the person I once was.'

'You have a gift for living, no matter how restrictive your circumstances. Whereas I'm entirely unsuited to it. Living for me can only be done in small doses. I tell myself it's because all my energy goes into my work, but perhaps it's also a form of cowardice.'

She smiled. 'It's why you are a great artist, and I a mere dilettante!'

'I understand finding the time and space to work is more difficult for a woman. The problem for me is to find some place where I can write. I cannot live in Germany. I find it repulsive, and the revulsion I feel has spread even to the language.'

'But how can you write in another language, even if you're fluent, without sacrificing your own voice?'

'If I were in Paris I could... Perhaps talking with you, I shall come closer to it.'

His words made her giddy. She knew he was leaving for Germany in three days, but for the moment all that mattered was to be sitting together in the sunshine beside that sparkling lake.

In the event he delayed his departure. She tried to tell herself his decision had nothing to do with her, though in her heart she did not believe it. They met a few times to walk or take coffee in one of the cafés. Once she invited him to supper, a simple meal because she couldn't afford anything fancy, but he seemed to relish it and was perfectly at home amongst the clutter of books, toys and art materials that littered the apartment. Despite his talk of longed-for isolation, he appeared to delight in the company of people who cared for him and, unlike Erich, the boys' exuberance amused rather than irritated him. When sometimes she joined in their games and the noise threatened to get out of hand, he merely clapped his hands and laughed aloud, as if enchanted by the mayhem.

One afternoon, when the children were out and they were alone together, he asked if he could read her something he was working on to hear her opinion of it. She did her best to empty her mind and concentrate on the sounds and rhythms of his language. When he had finished, she seized his hands and held onto them, unable to find words for the emotions that choked her.

At the end of the following week, she and the boys were due to visit friends in Beatenberg near Lake Thun, and René was still in Geneva. She had been looking forward to visiting her friends but as long as he remained she could not bear to leave. Against every instinct she forced herself to be practical. It was too late now to change plans and the boys were so much looking forward to the visit. Above all, a sudden change of arrangements would imply that she expected something more from René than she had grounds to hope for.

On the afternoon before their departure he came over to bid them goodbye, bringing for the journey some of the little cakes they all loved, elegantly presented in a white box tied with pink ribbon. Unable to restrain their excitement, the boys suggested eating them there and then and Merline agreed. Whilst the children prepared a festive table and waited for the kettle to boil, she and Rilke stepped out onto the balcony.

The afternoon was warm and the air scented with lime blossom from the trees that lined the street.

'You must be sure to write as soon as you reach Beatenberg and say whether the cuckoo has arrived yet. I hear it comes early to that part of Switzerland,' he said.

Lowering her eyes from his gaze, she murmured her assent, throat too dry to speak. When she looked up he seized her hands, observing her with an intensity that made her look away, afraid of revealing what she felt. He reached out to touch her cheek, softly repeating her name. A moment later the children called them in to tea.

Beatenberg, 1919
Merline

Merline arrived in Beatenberg, cocooned in a happiness she could not have imagined. Like a moon circuiting its planet, her wanderings had finally led her to her destined course. Her friends, a sculptress and her female companion, lived in an abandoned schoolhouse with outhouses that provided studio space. The boys, set free, rejoiced wildly at their liberty.

As soon as he had settled down, Balthus began working on some illustrations to a Chinese novel with the declared intention of sending them when they were finished to René. It pleased her how readily the boy had taken to him, almost too eager for his praise. At night in the bed they shared, he asked her over and over again, 'Do you think René will like the drawings? Should I write a formal dedication or wait and see if he thinks they're any good?'

She took him in her arms and did her best to still his agitation until at length he fell asleep, curled within her embrace like a young animal. She loved the bony feel of his shoulder blades when she held him against her in their narrow bed. But his febrile temperament worried her. His mind was filled with adult questions about art and life, though his body despite his height was still a child's. She pressed her face into his neck as he slept, breathing in his odour. He would do great things in his life, of that she had no doubt, yet she feared for him.

A few days later they sent off a parcel of his drawings and he received a letter back from René by return. With great pride he read it aloud, repeating the most extravagant praises again and again until his brother Pierre tried to grab it off him, shouting that if he had to listen to the damn thing one more time he'd tear it into a thousand pieces. Merline ordered Balthus to hand the letter over to her for safekeeping but he ran off, brandishing it in his fist.

Later that day she took a basket of washing into the orchard to hang up the clothes to dry and caught sight of him crouched in the fork of a cherry tree. Still irritated from their earlier confrontation, she gave no sign of having seen him though she felt his gaze on her. The wind caught the sheet she was pegging onto the line and tangled her up in its damp embrace, exaggerating the contours of her breasts and thighs. A moment later the boy jumped down from the tree and, running past her, reached out an arm so that her basket tipped, emptying the last of the wet clothes onto the muddy ground.

These days he was even more full of pranks than usual. Mostly she put them down to childish high spirits but sometimes he seemed possessed by the devil. One morning she was scattering corn in the orchard for the hens and there was a fierce cackling from the henhouse. She hurried over to find that someone had left the door unlatched. The rooster had got inside and was trying to mount a furious broody hen. She knew who was responsible, though she said nothing. Chiding would only add to his mischief.

Whatever leisure she could snatch, she spent reading *The Book of Hours* that René had given her on her departure from Geneva. She thought of him constantly and dreamed of him too, both sleeping and waking. Nothing had ever moved her like the music of his verse, even when she didn't fully understand it. Her friends, Margret and Dora, commented with mild recrimination on her lack of sociability and the hours she spent walking or sitting alone. She replied that she was making the most of the warm weather to store up against the Berlin winter to come. She didn't mention René, though Balthus brought his name into almost every conversation. She knew they were hurt by her lack of frankness but she couldn't help it. There was so little to say.

A couple of days later a boy cycled up from the post office with a telegram from René in Berne. He asked if she could leave the boys with her friends for a few days and join him there. She ran straight to the station without speaking to any of the others, to find out the time of a train and send him a telegram by return.

When she got home she told Margret and Dora what she had done and begged their forgiveness for not having consulted them first. The sight of her bright eyes and rapturous face made it impossible for them to be angry, though they warned her to take things slowly. She barely took in their words but hugged them both in joyous gratitude, insisting she would only be gone for a couple of days and promising to bring back some of the city's famed chocolates for each member of the household.

On the train she gazed out of the window, barely seeing the vineyards and orchards heavy with ripening fruit on the slopes of passing hills. Despite its unexpectedness, she had known René's invitation would come. All her life she'd believed in the passion of love as the highest form of being. In recent years her faith had seemed a delusion, though she had never entirely lost it. Her marriage was proof, if that were needed, of the dangers of surrendering oneself to another. But this, she told herself, was different. Surrender to a higher being such as René was not submission so much as fulfilment of her destiny, and she welcomed whatever it would bring. It was not passion that killed but its absence. Loving him made her stronger and more alive, and from its abundance spilled greater love for everything that surrounded her.

René was waiting for her at the station. They dropped her bag at the hotel and set off arm in arm to explore the city. She knew very little of it other than the quarter where she had stayed with her brother's friends on first arriving in Switzerland. Now it was as though she was seeing everything for the first time. They wandered through cobbled streets and alleyways, pausing here and there at bookshops and small, tempting épiceries to sample the delicious things on offer. She felt the movement of his body against hers as they walked, and the warmth of his flesh through the sleeve of his jacket.

They dined at a small restaurant not far from the hotel and went to bed early. His room was on the top floor under the eaves. It had dark old-fashioned furniture and a mansard window overlooking the bustle of the street. She was shy about undressing in front of him and did so quickly when he had gone along the corridor to the bathroom, folding her clothes neatly onto a chair and slipping under the covers to await his return. Bitter memories of her husband's response to her nakedness reminded her how easily a woman who displayed herself immodestly could repel a man. And she and René knew one another so little.

But when at last he lay down beside her under the heavy quilt and drew her to him, running his hands at first tentatively over her body, all self-consciousness left her. The sexual act she'd come to dread because it left her more dissatisfied and alone than ever, transformed itself into a union of ecstatic fulfilment. And when it was over she lay quietly at his side, too full of happiness to sleep. The rise and fall of his breathing as he slept kept time with the beating of her heart.

For three days she continued in a state of bliss she'd not known could exist, wanting nothing but the moment. She did her best to imprint on her memory images of their room and the view over the rooftops so that no detail of touch, sight, sound or scent should ever be lost. Then as suddenly as it had begun, the visit was over. She found herself once more at the station remembering only minutes before the train left her promise to buy chocolates for the boys, which she managed to do from a kiosk next to the platform.

As the train pulled away, she watched René's figure grow smaller until with the bend of the track it disappeared altogether. She was seized with such an intense feeling of loss that her heart contracted in pain and she had to put her hand over her mouth to stop herself from crying out. She leaned her head back against the cushion and with her eyes closed began counting the hours until she might hope to see him again. The desert of time that stretched ahead rendered life meaningless. Even the prospect of seeing the children offered little comfort, and she wondered bitterly if it might have been better never to have come to Berne at all if the aftermath was to suffer like this.

As soon as she got back to the schoolhouse, she shut herself away to write to René a barely coherent account of her thoughts:

Often I dream and in my dreams I see myself with you — far, far away on a long journey. Oh, René, René, blessings on you! For seeing me before you when you leave me: as a fountain, a tree, a flower, in your star shining above you — for you. I have kissed Balthus and told him; 'this comes from far away'.

She received a reply by return of post:

It was your body which was the miraculous equivalent of that fountain, for it too leaps up, and all the infinite nostalgia it has ever felt has served only to enrich the intensity of its fall, which is the strength of your arms. And I remember certain gestures of a grace so complete that they too were like that fountain, and your smile itself, never lost, that returns again to your mouth. How rich you are, my friend, with that wealth which can never be counted, for it is the wealth of nature, a blessed store that is transformed without ever being depleted.

She read and reread the letter and carried it with her in her pocket. Each day she wrote to him, sometimes twice, and received as many replies in return. She was far out to sea and Margret and Dora gave up trying to reach her. She carried out her chores and did her best to join in the usual household activities but her mind seemed always absent. Pierre responded by becoming more self-contained than ever. Balthus on the other hand was aggressive and affectionate by turns and always demanding. At one moment he playfully wooed her attention; the next he grew venomously critical.

He too wrote regularly to René but refused to show her his replies, insisting they were for his eyes alone. He was growing secretive and the violence of his feelings at times alarmed her. It was only through Dora that she discovered he'd been making a series of drawings with captions about his little cat, Mitsou, which had gone missing in Geneva. He told Dora he intended sending them to René as soon as they were finished. Hitherto, he had always sought Merline's opinion first. Now he bypassed her entirely and his exclusion hurt her deeply. She mentioned to Dora and Margret her fear that René's lavish praises encouraged the tyrannical side of Balthus' nature. Then suddenly his mood would change and he came running to her, full of enthusiasm about some model or drawing he'd just finished. He flung his arms around her so violently that the two of them lost their balance and collapsed together onto a chair in a heap of laughter.

Geneva, 1919
Merline

Shortly after their return to Geneva, Balthus joined his brother at the Lycée Calvin and Merline attempted to get down to some serious work. Once they were back in the apartment, the children took up so much of her time she had scarcely an hour in the day for work. There had been a time in Paris before motherhood when, like René, she believed art to be the most important thing in her life. Now she saw her ability to consider herself an artist further compromised, and in a moment of recklessness she suggested to René that she might send the boys to live with her sister Gina in Berlin for a while. He pointed out as tactfully as he could that such a plan would suit neither her sons nor himself, and that he was sure after a short time it would not suit her either. Solitude was the price he must pay for his work and since the boys already saw very little of their father, they could scarcely be expected to do without their mother too. She accepted the logic of his words, but raged against the trap she'd made for herself.

He departed for his lodgings in Beatenberg, leaving her to make do with letters and long hours lost in daydreams, oblivious to her sons' demands. She knew that for him love might fuel the engine of his creativity but domesticity destroyed it, though that did not make enduring his terms any easier. He felt no guilt regarding the daughter he corresponded with and occasionally sent money to but almost never met. He made it clear that in his eyes one of Merline's strengths was her acceptance of his need for solitude, unlike other women he'd known. And as she herself had sworn as much, now she must stand by it.

What was hardest to bear was her realisation of how much easier he found it to accommodate the demands of her two young sons than her own. In his eyes doing what he could for them was the best way of supporting her, and how could she disagree? In Paris she might have found a way to accept his conditions without resentment. But here in this no-man's-land, without visas, money or any foreseeable future, forced to beg charity from whosoever would give it, her love was all that sustained her. Even her desire for lovemaking was often refused during the brief visits that every few weeks were all he allowed. He needed to conserve his strength, and she persuaded herself it was enough to lie in his embrace and listen to a recitation of the thoughts that preoccupied him. But when she returned home such meagre rewards did little to make up for the starvation of waiting.

As money ran out, the need for her and her children to return to Berlin grew ever more pressing. Seeing the desperation of her situation and with nothing to offer her himself, René wrote to one of his rich patrons asking her to take in Merline and her sons. Merline could act as housekeeper, and the boys, who were both fluent in three languages and exceptionally talented, would be worthy companions to the great lady's own children. When he told her what he'd done, she agreed. Though the prospect appalled her, it was surely preferable to returning to the city she loathed. But when the great lady replied that she was planning a trip and therefore had no need of anyone at present, she felt nothing but relief.

In the meantime René had found a publisher for Balthus' book of drawings, which was to be entitled *Mitsou*, and promised to write an introduction for it. Merline expressed her gratitude for all his efforts on their behalf. She had known from the start this was how life with René would be, yet in her darkest moments she could not deny the bitterness she felt at his refusal to grant her the one thing she longed for. It made little difference to remind herself that she was a married woman with two children, and as long as she was tied to Erich nothing could change. She knew that were she free René would behave no differently.

In his absence she treasured his letters, together with every gift and trivial memento he'd ever sent her. Balthus described their apartment as a shrine to René, complete with bunches of wilted flowers that remained in their vases long after they had faded. Living there, he declared, was like living in a station waiting room in permanent expectation of a train, which, like René, never came. She chided him for his impertinence, but could not deny the aptness of his words.

René wrote to her:

My most dear, tell me, do I sustain you so badly that in spite of all my loving help you let yourself fall into such terrible misbelief in life? I am not reproaching you for it, I suffer with you, that's all, and rather than make a useless attempt at false consolation, tell you that I understand you. I understand — none could do so better — your oppression, your distress and how at times you feel forsaken by all the strength that grew from the contact of our fiery lives. My friend, if our separation were so great a wrong, do you think it would have been forced upon us? What makes it so painful is that we are both unable to enrich it with all the true consequences of our prodigious happiness. If you were alone now (as you yourself wrote the other day) you could have created a quite different consciousness for yourself, valiant and consenting. I too am bewildered for want of solitude and concentration. I am obliged to see people and talk all day.

I know very well all that I am saying here imposes a very unequal burden upon us two; you are too much of a woman not to suffer infinitely under that postponement of love which this task seems to imply. Moreover, in gathering my whole self together around my work, I am assuring myself of the means to my most abiding happiness; whilst you — at the present moment at least — when you turn towards your life, you find it encumbered by half-petrified duties. Do not let me discourage you, dearest. You may be sure that all this will change. The transfiguration of your heart will itself enable you to influence, little by little, the obstinate facts of reality. All that seems impenetrable to you now will be rendered transparent by your burning heart. Do not dwell on it at this moment, and forbid yourself to judge life during these hours of obscurity that prevent you from seeing its true expanse.

P.S. When I go out I always wear the gloves you washed for me and when I take them off, my hands feel your hands, your soap, your little basin and the air of your balcony.

She read his letter over many times, surrendering herself to his words, though they did nothing to alter the 'obstinate facts of reality'.

A few days later in an attempt to prove that despite everything her time had not been wasted, she sent him some sketches she had been working on. He wrote to her by return:

I've lighted a splendid fire, the first for a week, and by the light of the logs burning passionately, I am looking at your pastels in love with everything that I have just unpacked. One loses oneself in them, it's magical, there's no resisting them. The golden hair of the girl on the balcony of spring takes on a sensual sheen, it's really a whole season of puberty making use of it to seduce. And the girl imagines it's only herself! There's a flickering going on as there is in my fire, the darkness glows and the light darkens somehow into itself like a northern summer night… And the Woman at the Mirror, so rich, so 'dreamed'; how well she shows her entanglement with the mirror… And the Pretty Sleeper, yes, as a woman she is pretty, as a work of art she is sublime!

On and on he went for pages, extolling the witchcraft of her pencil in its ability to capture the inner truth of her subject through its outward form. She drank in his praises, trying not to think they were also an attempt to compensate her for his absence.

His letters were lifelines yet they made no difference to her situation. Each day it grew more desperate, together with her health. Either she must find employment or return to her family in Germany. With winter setting in the rheumatism she suffered from was also growing worse, as though inner suffering manifested itself in bodily pain. She longed to get away on her own for a few weeks, perhaps to a sanatorium where she could rest and her health might improve. But Christmas was approaching and how could she afford it?

She wrote to René:

I wonder if I have the strength to change my dress and be festive. Ah, I am tired unto death and the best fate would be to go to bed without care, all alone, and sleep, sleep perhaps until the end of the world.

Two days later she received a parcel from him full of presents for Christmas and accompanied by a long letter. She wrote back at once:

My darling, your parcel and things have arrived. I first read the long letter and truthfully as you wanted I put the parcel in the cupboard to wait for Christmas Eve. Yesterday, I swore not to tell the children that a parcel from Beatenberg had arrived. But as soon as they came back, before I had time to reflect, my mouth had betrayed me and we had begun to undo it. Chéri, I thank you for your great, great kindness in having thought of us. You are so good, so good, and, René, this night I did not go to sleep except between 2 and 4am. I was so close, so close to you that I was shaken with passion like a tree in a great wind. It was a storm, René, that as I dreamed would come again whenever I wanted it to. It was so vivid, oh, unimaginable, my darling. Have you felt it?

We have time, we are still young, aren't we? René, we are not old. Darling, I've so much, so much to say to you. I will tell you all when I come to you, leaning against you as I kneel before you and you will hold my head between your two tender hands. Feel me, oh, feel me, my love. I fly towards you like a butterfly without body or weight, which dances its love around a beloved bird.

But as Christmas drew nearer the euphoria receded, and her pains returned worse than ever. Her suffering cast a pall over the household and as if in response Balthus fell ill with fever. He had already missed so much school he might not be able to take the end of year exam. Merline put him to sleep in her bed and the world closed in on them. She knew that in recent months her self-absorption had made her neglect her children, but however hard she sought it her old resilience eluded her.

On Christmas Eve, determined at least to make the celebration a joyous one, she rallied her strength and summoned Pierre to accompany her on a last minute shopping expedition. As they emerged onto the dark streets, she looked up at the sky filled with stars.

'See, how lovely it is!' she cried out in joy.

Pierre's heart lifted too. He raised his face to the heavens, but said nothing for fear of puncturing the fragile bubble of his mother's elation.

For the whole evening her euphoria subsisted, spreading a blessed warmth over the three of them. At midnight she went to the door to let in the Yuletide 'King' and declared joyfully she had the strangest feeling it was René who had come to join them. The children, delighted, made a show of welcoming in the imaginary guest with deep bows and salaams.

Afterwards, Balthus, still weak from flu, returned to the divan in the living room and watched as his mother and Pierre lit the candles in the seven-branched menorah and on the tree, beneath which she had laid out the presents. She had managed to save at least some of René's gifts for this moment and they opened them one by one in a mood of solemn excitement. She gasped aloud when she saw the bracelet of exquisite blue stones lying in its bed of white velvet he had sent her. But the gift that delighted her most was a book of his sonnets. She held it in her hands and all fear and resentment evaporated in a rush of love and gratitude.

She wrote to him at once the following day, determined to erase the image of the ungrateful burden she feared she had become with her endless litany of money and domestic problems:

But now something serious. This letter from you this morning has seriously displeased me, dear. Since when do you fill these pages so precious to me, above all as they come as rarely as violets in winter time, with speaking to me of household matters? No, no, no! It is to efface my wretched Christmas letter that I am quickly writing this one. I see what a grave fault I have committed and you, my dear, dear René, are contaminated by it already. Dear one, dear one, embrace me. You do it too little. I say to you it is much more necessary to my life than it would be to any wretched girl. If I weren't ashamed of my age, I would jump around you like some crazy young thing, dragging you with me until we collapsed together onto some soft cushions and then you would no longer think that I am ill.

I beg you, René, seriously, believe me as a friend, that never, never, never have I counted on you in any way. What gives me so much pain is these misconceptions. You do not need to say to me that you will be poor for a long time to come. One couldn't be poorer than I am and I never looked for riches, so do not speak of that.

But she was unable to sustain the pretence of being restored to her old self, and by New Year was on the brink of despair from the pain caused by her rheumatism. She could no longer hide from the children, or from René in the rare moments they were together, that every movement had become torture. The children did their best to help out with chores, and each day Balthus brought her some small gift such as a blue jay's feather or a sprig of winter flowering cherry to raise her spirits. It was no good. She must have rest and the only way to ensure that was a stay in a sanatorium.

She wrote to René:

Be sure, my dear, I shall be well looked after. It is necessary, I see it now. I am broken and you would weep if you could see my poor body cramped beneath this terrible suffering. But that will pass, my love. Think, oh, think of me and I will think of you and when you call me, don't dare imagine this sickness… I want to forget everything, my name, my house, my family, to disappear in you, my darling. You are my homeland. I want to forget even that I know how to speak and to hear nothing but the blood and beating of our two hearts.

Her words would only add to the burden she'd become, but she no longer cared. Without him she had no resting place and her life was permanent exile.

Berlin, 1994
Eli

I want to forget everything… to disappear in you, my darling.
You are my homeland.

Merline's words filled Eli with a mixture of compassion and chill. Her repetitions and false starts were evidence of the intensity of her emotion as she struggled to accept the starvation rations on which she, like all Rilke's women, was kept. She did her best to respect his demand for solitude, but suffering and humiliation frequently got the better of her, though she knew rebellion had no chance of success. Her helpless dependency was a dire warning, if such were needed, against obsessive love being one's raison d'être. Rilke demanded of whoever cared for him to surrender to his higher purpose and she acquiesced. In doing so she became the author of her own miseries. It was impossible not to be swept up by her passion and determination to live life as though it might match up to her dreams. Yet the bitter truth remained that denying herself the possibility of becoming the artist she might have been rendered her suffering in the end commonplace. However heroic her self-sacrifice, it meant nothing in the eyes of her famous son or the world, to whom she was a woman of no importance, a mere footnote in the lives of two great men.

The magazine agreed to pay modest expenses for an article on 'Die Neue Wilden', a group of Berlin artists whose fame had spread to Britain and America.

'And while you're about it, you could see how the new Jewish Museum's coming along,' Michael said. 'Quite a talking point, I hear!'

With the money she'd saved she could stay for at least a month. She booked herself into a small hotel and called Gunter to tell him of her plan. He welcomed her return but warned her his time would be taken up with his film, scheduled now to go into production in the autumn. They'd both be busy, she replied, and would see each other when they could. She arranged for a friend to take over her flat during her absence and to look after the cat.

He was waiting for her at Schonefeld airport in the former East of the city. She saw him amongst the waiting crowd, peering rather short-sightedly having forgotten his glasses, and her heart lifted. They embraced and made their way through the busy concourse to the car park. His silence as he negotiated his way out of the airport through diversions and half-finished roads, made her tense. But when eventually they emerged onto the main highway, moving slowly through heavy traffic, he turned to her and smiled.

'Sorry! I haven't been very welcoming. It takes all my concentration to find my way out of that damned place. The chaos just gets worse!'

'It's not what one expects from a German airport!'

He laughed. 'Maybe the trains once ran on time in Berlin, but not any more.'

'How's the film?'

'We've finally got the money. We start shooting in the new year, so there's a lot to be done.'

She asked about Malawi, where the film was to be be made.

'It's one of the poorest African countries, despite being rich in natural resources. The average age of its population is sixteen, largely due to Aids.'

Eli listened to him as she gazed out of the window at the neat rows of villas with their carefully tended gardens, still firmly stuck in the communist era a world away from the shabby vibrancy of the centre.

He laid his hand on her knee. 'I'm doing all the talking. Tell me what you've been up to.'

'Nothing much. For the time being I've put Balthus on hold and am looking at Germany.'

'I'm sorry I didn't manage to get back to you when you called from your parents'.'

'It wasn't important. I was at a cousin's bat mitzvah and it all got a bit much. I needed to speak to someone from the outside world.'

'I didn't realise you were religious.'

Something in his tone made her bristle.

'I'm not. It was a family celebration. Do you disapprove of that?'

'I'm German. Our history makes me suspicious of tribes. It's why I choose to inhabit this island of dissenters.'

'Berlin's no longer an island. It's the capital.'

Sensing her hostility, he softened.

'You're right, of course. Something I do my best to ignore. Since the fall of the Soviet Union and the Wall, we're again becoming obsessed with national identity.'

'After the war my grandparents used to attend meetings about world government, to put an end to such things forever. Nowadays most young people in Britain don't even bother to vote.'

'If my son's anything to go by, politics doesn't interest the young here either.'

'What interests him, then?'

It was the first time he'd mentioned his son.

'Music. Like most young people.'

'Ah, dreams to become a rock star!'

'I guess so.'

He switched the subject to a Taiwanese film they might see that evening.

The following morning she showered and dressed but decided not to take breakfast in the dreary hotel dining room. She planned to spend the morning visiting the site for the new Jewish Museum and to stop at a café on the way. The guidebook said that before the war there'd been half a million Jews living in Berlin. Today there were around 12,000. Perhaps, gradually, they were returning.

In one of Merline's letters to Rilke written in the early 1920s, she'd thanked him for including 'my poor old father' in his Christmas gifts as though it were a special kindness. With hindsight Eli realised that was most likely a reference to the rising tensions concerning Jews. Her grandparents had rarely spoken about the Berlin period of their lives, and she didn't even know which part of the city they'd inhabited. She wished now she'd been more curious, before it was too late.

It was a bright morning as she emerged from the U-Bahn and crossed the street. She could hear music coming from the direction of the Museum. As she rounded the corner, she saw a couple of big open-sided trucks parked in a small square surrounded by a crowd of noisy people. A group of musicians was playing punk music on one of the trucks while some girls gyrated wildly on the other. The young men wore black t-shirts, combat trousers and heavy boots; the girls were dressed wholly in black. Some of them had shaved heads and faces and ears festooned with piercings. The crowd around the trucks was bouncing up and down, waving beer cans and shouting. A few had dogs with studded collars entwined with German flags, which barked or howled at the mayhem.

The quickest way to the museum was through the square but Eli hesitated when she saw a group of protesters with placards approaching from the far side. They were chanting and throwing leaflets into the crowd, which the shaven-headed youths trampled underfoot or picked up and with them made gestures of wiping their arses. Scuffles were breaking out and though most people's attention was still on the band, it looked as if things would pretty soon turn ugly.

She pulled her camera from her pocket and began snapping the scene. Surprisingly she seemed to be the only one taking pictures. One of the musicians on the truck spotted her as she drew closer and began capering about for the camera like some crazy monkey as he plucked manically at his guitar. The crowd, delighted, roared their appreciation. More and more people with placards were streaming into the square from the direction of the station and she could hear police sirens in the distance. Having no desire to get caught up in a riot, Eli grabbed a couple more shots and made off down a side street.

In the evening when she arrived at Gunter's apartment, she related the incident to him as he prepared spaghetti vongole for supper.

'At first it seemed like a party. Quite jolly!'

'Jolly! You realise those people were neo-Nazis?'

'Well, by the look of them the old lot would have been thoroughly ashamed!'

'I'm afraid they're far from a joke.'

'You think they were there because of the museum?'

'I've no doubt of it. They don't need much of an excuse.'

He drained the pasta from the boiling water.

'They're like a disease in our blood that can't be cured. My parents became communists because they believed it would put an end to fascism. Now the Wall's down the whole thing's starting again.'

He set down a steaming plate next to the salad on the table and invited her to take a seat.

'I took some photos.'

She passed him her camera.

'Serve yourself.'

He ran through the pictures then exclaimed, 'Jesus Christ!'

'What is it?'

He replaced the camera on the table without a word and served himself. But instead of eating, he poured another glass of wine, lit a cigarette, and went over to the open window. Smoke drifted back into the room, with the sound of voices from the street below. She tried to concentrate on her food, but his silence made it impossible.

'Please, Gunter! What's wrong?'

He returned to the table and sat down. When he spoke, it was clear that each word cost him effort.

'That boy on the truck with the guitar... He's my son. Bruno.'

'My God! Are you sure? I mean he's pretty far away.'

'D'you think I don't know my own son?'

She said nothing, too stunned to reply.

'I'm sorry... I didn't mean to snap.'

'Did you know he was involved with... those people?

He shook his head. 'For over a month he's not been turning up when we're supposed to meet.' His voice was tight with anger.

'Did he say why?'

'He made excuses, like having to rehearse with the band he was playing with. I thought they were just a group of unsavoury punks. All my life there's only been one enemy. And now my son has joined them!'

'Perhaps they are just punks. Not real Nazis.'

'All Nazis are real!'

She meant to say that in Britain almost nobody took the BNP seriously, though perhaps the comparison wasn't entirely helpful. There were some, like her own father, who believed the nightmare had never gone away. And here was Gunter's son proving them right.

'I changed his nappies, taught him to ride a bike, swim, took him fishing, helped him with his homework... How could it have come to this?'

His expression was grim in a way that seemed to age him ten years. She tried to imagine what it must feel like to discover one's own child had become the enemy.

'You knew nothing about all this? I mean, there were no warning signs?'

He shook his head. 'Not that I was alert enough to notice.'

They sat in silence, until at length she got up and went over to him. She put her arms around him, feeling the rigidity in his body that refused to let go.

Geneva, 1921
Merline and Balthus

During the spring of 1921, barely a month after she had returned to Geneva from the sanatorium, Merline's financial situation became so desperate she had no money even for a third-class train ticket to Berg for one of the snatched visits to René that she lived for. Her sister was unable to lend her any since her own situation, she declared, was just as bad. Merline could no longer hide from herself that it was time to leave.

Though René was also beset with financial troubles, he managed to organise sufficient funds for her and the children to move back temporarily to their old apartment in Pré-Jérôme, but she could not rely on his charity forever.
He wrote to her from Berg:

> *My dear one, tomorrow if after you have taken your sister to Coravin, oh these eternal stations, when you return home I expect you will find a short word from me and that it will contribute in some way to help you to begin again your life alone with the children in the Pré-Jérôme on its old basis of confidence, which you had built so well and where, in its best moments, you found a happy equilibrium in spite of all the uncertainties about tomorrow or the future. Open it, my beloved friend, open the book of your heart, which I have worked to rekindle like a thousand and one nights, precious with all the ornaments my love can find*

from your rich treasure. Open up a new page, quite white with
hope, bright in the gleam of a loving and vital belief. Begin again,
my darling, and all your entourage will rejoice with you. In two
days Balthus will no longer regret that he stayed and Pierre,
the imperturbable judge, will assert in his rather ponderous and
vigorous words that this is a new beginning. You'll see.

It was a great relief to be back in the place where she had
once been so happy. But that didn't allay the fear of what was
to come, however much she tried to deny it. She wrote back:

Geneva is very deserted now, although beautiful. The town
makes me afraid. I scarcely dare go out further than the Place
Neuve. Balthus has just made a young page in wax about 17
years old. He has black eyes, very melancholy. His hair is all
black and he is perfectly beautiful. At the moment we are sewing
a costume worthy of his beauty. Before we put him to bed this
evening with great care, we placed him on his two fine legs so
that he will be able to take up strong, amorous postures and
look proudly about him. If one day he finds himself blessed
with a beautiful soul too, I shall not be surprised.

But what can I do in this entourage? René, make me some
sort of sign, I beg you, and tell me when I should be silent. God
in his way gives signs to the birds during a storm, and for me,
my darling, this is a bird's prayer. Make me quiet if that is
what is needed.

Whenever she had a spare moment she threw herself into her painting, working to the point where she collapsed with exhaustion in her armchair and fell asleep under the last rays of afternoon sun. When the children returned from school they woke her demanding supper, as if by refusing to acknowledge any weakness her health would be miraculously restored.

René kept up the flow of letters and books, but nothing could make up for his absence. With the small gift of money he included in one of them she bought a train ticket for a brief visit, which was all he allowed. She knew what her visits cost him, how each interruption set back his work by days. It shamed her that in her weakness it was she who was wearing him out with her demands, and as she boarded the train she swore to herself this would be the last.

His mother's distracted state and the precarious conditions of their lives made Balthus increasingly withdrawn and there was no one he could turn to. He was thirteen and with his peripatetic life had had little opportunity to make friends. The only person in whom he could confide was his brother, who criticised what he called his whining and refused to discuss his complaints. School offered nothing, and his teachers' impoverished concept of knowledge made it pointless as well as tedious. Most days he spent in the museum or wandered alone through the town, rummaging in secondhand bookshops in hope of a bargain. Only what he discovered for himself, and above all through René, had any meaning.

One morning at the beginning of March, Merline received a letter from the Public Instruction informing her that her son had left the Lycée. She waited impatiently for him to return at the usual time and challenged him at once. He admitted his truancy without the least sign of guilt.

'When my teacher, M. Pittard, confronted me with my absence, I told him I'd gone to live with my aunt.'

He laughed, expecting Merline to share the joke. But she saw nothing funny.

'Why tell such a lie?'

'Because there are so many better, more interesting ways to get an education!' he retorted.

Despite herself she could not disagree, and when he saw her softening he began strutting up and down in imitation of the pontificating schoolmaster and soon his sins were forgotten in laughter. He ran to fetch the work he'd been doing at the museum and laid it out before her. As always when she looked at his drawings, she was astonished by their skill and maturity.

A few days later she and Balthus were summoned to the school. As they walked along corridors smelling of wax and disinfectant on their way to the Director's office, Merline was reminded of her own schooldays. She listened to the masters' harsh voices barking out their tired instructions and the chorused responses of the pupils with a feeling of horror. When they entered the Director's study she looked around at its book-lined walls and oversized desk, that like their owner seemed designed to intimidate, and felt more admiration than censure for her son's rebellion. The trouble was that at barely thirteen the law required him to attend school for a good few more years.

The interview was concluded when she politely informed the Director that they were about to return to Berlin. He made no attempt to hide his relief and since this was most likely the last time he'd be seeing either of them, he made the gesture of accompanying them down to the entrance foyer.

In the hallway Merline paused in front of a pastel drawing that hung on the wall. The Director smiled.

'I fear I haven't complimented you, chère Madame, on the excellence of this piece. It was most generous of you to donate it to the school.'

She laughed, realising his mistake.

'Sir, the picture isn't my work. It's by Balthus!'

'Ah! I see…'

She watched in amusement as he struggled to disguise his discomposure.

But as soon as they'd turned the corner of the street, she confronted Balthus.

'Whatever possessed you to say that drawing was mine?'

'Then the school would value it more,' he replied earnestly. 'People like M. Pittard wouldn't even believe I exist if it wasn't for M. Rilke's preface to *Mitsou*.'

She reached out and hugged him to her.

'Dear son, how could anyone doubt your existence! Especially in this country of Calvin, that unlike you has so little time for pranks!'

She remembered how a fortune teller had once predicted Balthus' leap day birthday meant he was destined for great things. She had no need of fortune tellers to convince her how remarkable was her changeling child. But that only made it the more painful that their nomadic life offered him so few chances and placed such unfair burdens on his young shoulders, something her own suffering often made her forget.

Two weeks later the boys broke up from school, and she arranged a small farewell party for some of their friends. They decorated the apartment with candles and coloured branches, made masks out of papier-mâché and prepared delicious food for the seven guests. It was a long time since they'd had a celebration and she was determined to make it a jolly occasion. With such a warm welcome the guests soon forgot their shyness and when they had eaten every scrap of food, Merline cleared aside the plates and ordered the games to begin. When the guests finally left the three of them flopped down exhausted, proclaiming with united voice the evening to have been a triumph. Scarcely able to keep her eyes open, Merline suggested they go to bed and leave the clearing up till morning.

Next day, as she surveyed the chaos of trampled food, spilt drink and overturned furniture, including her broken watch discovered in the seat of the armchair, she knew that nothing now could delay their departure.

Berlin, 1921
Merline

In Germany inflation continued to spiral ever upwards and finding a school for the boys was well-nigh impossible, let alone paying for it. It was decided that Pierre should stay on in Geneva *en pension* and continue his studies at the Lycée. He was sixteen and sensible, unlike her younger son. Friends would keep an eye on him and René had promised to remain in close touch. He also pledged himself to provide funds for Balthus' school fees in Berlin, though Merline had no idea where he would find the money.

They arrived in Berlin on a wet April afternoon. The first things that struck her were the throngs of idlers standing around on street corners and the raucous shouts and laughter that spilled forth from the bars and cafés that had sprung up since her last visit. The city felt poised between torpor and a frenzied attempt to deny the panic that had seized the nation. Everywhere the war was visible in the disfigured soldiers with their truncated limbs and shabby uniforms festooned with medals, holding out their begging bowls. As she fumbled in her purse for a spare pfennig she could ill afford, Merline averted her gaze from their mutilated features to spare them further pain. Balthus, on the other hand, stared at them with open curiosity. When she reprimanded him, he retorted that they wanted to be looked at, since forcing people to pay attention to their deformities was the only revenge for their suffering.

But worst of all were the skinny girls in cheap gaudy clothes, hanging on the arm of some thick-necked man old enough to be their grandfather, in the hope of enough money to pay next week's rent or at least a square meal. She longed to cry out that their youth deserved better, but necessity drove too hard a bargain in this dreadful place. Whatever soul the city once possessed had been consumed by the war. Now there was only disillusionment and the oblivion of the coming night. It was the last place to bring an impressionable boy.

She re-entered her brother and sister-in-law's flat with a dismal sense of déjà vu, a feeling she knew was shared by her hosts. Such dependence took away the last shreds of her dignity, and however much she tried to show gratitude by skivvying, nothing could make up to her sister-in-law for the intrusion.

After a few weeks she hadn't managed even the smallest drawing, and their life in the Rue Pré-Jérôme appeared as a distant dream. Each day was consumed with scraping together the astronomical sums needed to buy a loaf of bread, some leathery chunk of meat and a few tired vegetables. At night when she lay in bed she put her hands over her ears to block out the sounds that came through the wall of the neighbour's drunken shouts and his wife's sobbing, as she begged him to leave her a few pfennigs to feed the children. Relations between men and women had been reduced to a bare-knuckle fight.

A similar rivalry began to infect the children. Balthus, who hated the city almost as much as Merline did, was growing increasingly introverted and difficult. He seemed to take pleasure in tormenting his small cousin and when Merline chided him for it, he retorted that he was doing the kid a favour. How would he survive when he went to school if he didn't start toughening up? For the umpteenth time she asked herself what this life was doing to her son.

One night she put her head around the door of the child's bedroom and saw the terrified little boy sitting bolt upright in bed, eyes fixed on two puppets that pranced and capered in the light of the bedside lamp throwing grotesque shadows onto the wall. Behind them she made out the manipulating figure of Balthus. She ordered him to stop what he was doing at once, and took the child in her arms. But it was a long time before he grew calm enough to sleep.

Later that night, when they were both in bed, she chided Balthus, who insisted it was only a game. He went on to relate the tale he'd been enacting with such comic gusto that Merline forgot her anger in laughter. In the morning, however, she recalled the incident with shame, wondering if she too was becoming infected by the malevolence of this place.

A couple of nights later he was once again in the little boy's room, making his marionettes caper and gibber and sending the child's great dark eyes in his delicate face of a Roman putto wide with terror. This time she refused all excuses as she ordered Balthus out of the room, and threatened to tell her brother of his behaviour. She understood her son less and less. One moment he seemed indifferent to her anger, the next he demanded in an injured tone what he had done to make her stop loving him, and with an expression so innocently hurt she found it impossible to chide him.

Another night, when everyone was asleep, she woke to find him once again missing from their bed, and quickly went in search of him. As she opened the door of the child's bedroom, the shaft of light fell on him and he started up guiltily. He was kneeling beside the narrow cot of the young nurse from the Tegernsee who looked after the little boy, his face resting against the girl's plump bosom as it rose and fell with her breathing.

The following day he explained to her that he'd been conducting an experiment. By chance he'd heard the girl talking in her sleep and decided to record what she said. The trouble was she spoke an incomprehensible dialect interspersed with hearty chuckles, neither of which he knew how to write down. However comical his antics, she knew such behaviour would not be tolerated if her brother or sister-in-law were to learn of it. Her son was now thirteen and the girl a buxom eighteen-year-old.

Whenever they were alone together Balthus talked of René and how much he missed their conversations in this city of criminals and conmen.

'No one here cares for art, or any of the things that matter!' he declared.

His remark suggested the ideas and confidences he and she had once shared no longer meant anything, and she wondered if she should send him to his father in Munich. But that would mean having to ask Erich for the train fare and to fend off his repeated insistence that it would be more economical for them both to live there with him.

Balthus absented himself more and more but she said nothing. His usual excuse was that he'd stayed late at the library, having nowhere to do his homework at the flat. René might have been able to advise her, but she had burdened him enough with troubles he could do nothing about. Her letters had turned into self-pitying rants against the conditions of her daily existence so that in the end she usually threw away what she had written, unwilling to let the poison of her misery contaminate their relationship. Once or twice in an outburst she couldn't contain she gave rein to despair, asking herself bitterly why she should shield him from the realities of her existence whilst he lived in ease in Switzerland. She recalled the time he'd declared the love experience to be just 'a stunted, unfit subsidiary of the creative experience, almost its degradation'. Such words reduced her very being to something without value.

In response to one of her more anguished outbursts, he wrote:

It is heartbreaking to see you giving way to the idleness of a harmful sadness which does not even furnish you with dreams. I should be easy in my mind if I knew you were taking responsibility for your own life, as you did all the time in Geneva with such admirable energy; do you wish to crush me under the weight of the suspicion that it is I who have destroyed in you that youthful impulse, joyous in spite of everything?

The letter did little to assuage her anguish. 'Am I supposed to deny even my despair in order to give you comfort?' she asked herself.

In his next letter he wrote of how much he was looking forward to the imminent visit of his close friend and patron, the Princess Marie von Thurn und Taxis, and her anger boiled over. Though she had never met the illustrious lady, she knew she embodied all the culture and privilege René so valued in contrast to the vulgar distractions of the heart. He had let slip remarks that made it clear she was one of his benefactors who regarded her, Merline, as little better than a succubus who consumed his energies and threatened his work. She could picture the two of them, strolling arm in arm beside the river at Beatenberg, or seated under a weeping elm in the late afternoon sunshine, the Princess delivering in her measured tones the perspicacious comments he valued no less than the precious financial support she provided. How could she, Merline, demanding and ill-educated, hope to rival such a companion?

She wrote to him:

May 22nd 1921, Berlin

I am feeble, feeble in everything, René. I have no place. I am a reed balanced in one hand or rather an uprooted thing which has no home anywhere and I no longer have any character. I am like someone one locks up in an empty room and who eternally bangs her head against the four walls. I am prepared like Esther for these months of summer without you. I do not know these places you speak to me about, René, but since you consider me like a sick person I will only see you as my guardian. No, no, no, no! You know that these many months I have wanted to see you and love you. I have wanted to live near you. It is the pain of using up my heart and soul on notepaper. I understand very well that the presence of your princely friend makes mine impossible. I hope that your meeting together proves useful for your future.

Spring came at last and whenever returning bouts of lumbago permitted, she took time off from her domestic duties to work with the children in the local kindergarten. Their enthusiasm and inventiveness, untainted as yet by their surroundings, was as important as the pittance she earned, and did much to revive her spirits. By saving every pfennig, and with the prospect of having soon to leave her brother's flat, she had almost enough to return to Geneva for a couple of months, and to see Pierre.

Relieved at the prospect of their departure, her brother lent her the rest of what she needed to buy fares for Switzerland. She was to take the train via Munich and pick up Balthus, who'd been spending a few days with his father helping with sets for a Chinese play the theatre was putting on. Throughout the journey she fought her terror that something would force her back, if not Erich then border control. But as the train pulled into Munich, Balthus was waiting alone on the station platform. Erich, it turned out, was too busy with his production to concern himself with her movements.

At the border the usual scrutiny of papers caused further delay, but at last the guard blew his whistle and the train moved ponderously forward, releasing Balthus' tongue. He broke into a stream of eager prattle, describing his activities at the theatre and the sketches he'd sent to René. But as they gathered speed he fell silent again, until at length he declared, 'Not even you, Maman, can be more relieved than I am to be leaving Germany!

Switzerland, 1921
Merline

As soon as they arrived, she received a letter from René telling her that he was urgently looking for somewhere more permanent to live. A sawmill had opened up not far from the house he'd been loaned, working from six in the morning until eight and sometimes ten at night, every day except Sunday. The incessant whining of the machines grated on every nerve and destroyed all hope of concentration. She knew how obsessive he was about the intrusion of the least noise. It was clearly impossible for him to remain there and, most important, the situation offered her the opportunity to make herself useful.

Without further consideration she packed Balthus off to stay with her friends in Beatenberg, and prepared to join René in the search for a house. They selected as a base an old priory covered with climbing roses, whose scent wafted in through their bedroom window in the evenings after the dew had fallen.

The weather was glorious and in the morning they took breakfast on the terrace, which had a clear view to the hills. As if by magic Merline's ailments disappeared, and with them the bitterness that had accumulated in Berlin so that she was filled with a sense of wellbeing she'd thought lost. For once she was not merely the recipient of René's generosity, but the means by which he might achieve what he so badly needed and could not provide for himself.

Each morning as soon as she got up, she set about preparing an itinerary for the day. But finding a suitable property in a peaceful enough location was proving harder than anticipated. Several of the houses they saw were in urgent need of repair or too dilapidated to be renovated. Others had been done up tastelessly, or were too close to a main road or working farm and could never come up to René's demanding requirements. As he became increasingly discouraged, she refused to be put off. Now and then her enthusiasm even revived him and a visit he'd been dreading turned into a pleasant outing. But bit by bit she too was growing dispirited at their lack of success.

They moved on to Sierre and took rooms in the Hotel Bellevue, where they had often stayed before. Here, too, every place was either too expensive or had just been taken. Until, on the day before they'd decided to leave in despair of finding anything suitable, they took their usual after dinner stroll through town. Merline paused to look in a hairdresser's window and her eye fell on a photograph posted there. It showed a dilapidated thirteenth-century tower offered for sale or rent. Though at first glance it seemed entirely unlikely, she felt in her bones that this one was worth seeing.

They arranged a visit for the following morning and had difficulty finding the place. Several times they stopped to ask for directions, but at last they rounded a hill and there it was. The tower was the colour of warm earth, set against the greens and russets of orchards that fell away below. It had no electricity, running water or proper sanitation, but there was a view across vineyards to wooded hills with no sign of human habitation. They knew their search was over.

Whilst René rested in the shade of the building, Merline wandered around the overrun garden. It was a wilderness full of bees and butterflies that circled the roses tumbling in chaotic profusion over a colonnade and filling the air with their scent. This at last was the paradise she'd been seeking.

But securing the property proved unexpectedly difficult. The owner began having doubts about selling, and there were long drawn out negotiations which would have broken the patience of anyone less determined. Meanwhile, the funds René had been promised from one of his benefactors to help with the purchase and cover costs of conversion were also not forthcoming. On top of that there was the question of whether the place could ever be made habitable.

Merline was undeterred. She used the delays to draw up plans and seek out builders and craftsmen who could carry out the heavy work, and hired a team of workmen from the village to be ready at a moment's notice and some local women to help with the clean-up. At length, with diplomatic persistence, she managed to secure a lease.

Once work started she got down on hands and knees with the workmen, clearing rubble from floors and drains, and loving every minute of it. As the place began to take shape, the workers taught her how to plaster and decorate, skills that gave her even greater satisfaction than the choosing of curtains, furniture, linen, china, candles and what was needed to furnish the house in the comfort and style that meant so much to René. Never before had she had so much money to spend or worked so hard, and she had never been happier. Each day she rose early with no thought for aching limbs and roughened hands, eager for the day's tasks. At night she went to bed exhausted and slept till morning. As soon as the house was almost finished, she turned her attention to the garden.

By October the place was ready for René to move in. As he descended from the car and walked towards the building, she drank in his expression of astonished delight. She showed him round with undisguised pride, pointing out every lovingly crafted detail. And when he declared he couldn't have imagined such a transformation to be possible, she laughed with pleasure. This was the home he'd longed for and she had made it possible.

She had her own quarters upstairs and for the time being took on the domestic work until a suitable housekeeper could be found. René was particularly exigent about domestic arrangements and needed someone competent and sufficiently content with her own company to leave him alone. He told Merline repeatedly how grateful he was for what she had done for him. As a guest she would always be welcome. But he made it plain that he was planning a solid stint of work through the winter and for that he needed to be alone.

They invited Balthus over from Beatenberg, where he had spent the summer with her friends. She couldn't wait to show off the little kingdom she had created and to see his reaction, though for Balthus the pleasure was mixed. It wasn't easy to see his mother so proudly at home in a place where he was merely a guest. With René he always felt at ease. But when the three of them were together, he and Merline found themselves vying for René's attention like rivalrous siblings. She was not blind to this and tried as much as possible to leave the two of them alone for much of the day, busying herself in some other part of the house or garden. But she could not hide the relief she felt when Balthus returned to Beatenberg and she and René reverted to the harmony of their previous existence.

Gradually the leaves turned colour and fruits and berries ripened. She could feel René's growing impatience, and the faint hope he might ask her to stay faded. The summer had been a glorious interlude in her life, nothing more. After considerable searching she found a local girl who would make a suitable housekeeper, and spent a week training her. Then there was no further reason to delay. It was already November and René could wait no longer. She packed her bags, did her best to bid him an affectionate farewell, then she and Balthus set off once more for Berlin.

At Christmas René sent gifts, describing in his accompanying letter the beauty of the first snows at Muzot and the brilliance of the light. Cast out of Eden she wrote back to thank him, trying not to betray her anguish. A reticence was creeping into their letters, and for some time she had sensed his desire to withdraw from the intense intimacy they'd shared, as he had from all his previous lovers. She'd hoped the creation of Muzot, the embodiment of all he'd dreamed of, might put off that day. But it had not.

As winter ground on in Berlin, spring was in full bloom in Muzot. He wrote to her:

Nothing mean, nothing degrading has happened to us, to you, Beloved, but only something too great: if therefore any consolation were needed, let it be this… For the moment, Dearest, all that worries me is your health. Every morning that dawns in untold splendour amid so many roses, fills me with profound sadness because I cannot install you here on the terrace. How well you would feel in the sun, you would want for nothing, nothing, nothing. Yesterday the terrace, though so much smaller, reminded me of the one at Sierre. 'Look,' I said to you whom I felt quite near, 'look at the peonies with their wide-open red and pink wrappers, and the roses, the roses!' My Dearest, I'm showing you all this, not to make all your longing more unbearable but because to see the coming of summer is to show it to you; it means nothing to me otherwise.

His words served only to confirm her sense of exclusion and to inflame her longing.

Berlin, 1994
Eli

The day after his discovery of his son's involvement with neo-Nazis, Gunter asked Eli to move in with him and she agreed. His pain at discovering the son he loved had become part of what he most loathed, revealed an unexpected vulnerability for which she was almost grateful, and made her feel less of a passenger in his life.

The morning after her arrival in the flat was Saturday, and she woke with the sun shining in through the slats of the blinds. She got up, made coffee and returned to the bedroom with two mugs. Roused by smell of the coffee, Gunter, still half-asleep, heaved himself into a sitting position.

'It's beautiful out there. Perhaps we could take a river trip?' She handed him a mug.

'If that's what you'd like. I'm all yours today!'

'One of those boats with a buffet so we can have lunch.'

'I'd rather take you to a Russian place that's just opened near the Wasserturm.'

'OK!'

The boat took them along the Spree, past tree-lined streets and grassy banks, where people sprawled in the sunshine. They sat hand in hand in the prow of the boat, feeling the breeze on their faces. Strange, she thought, that this city, which for Merline had been a place of chaos and fear, was for her a place of joy. Moving gently over the water on this glorious morning, her lover at her side, she wanted nothing more than to observe the play of light on water and to hear the birdsong.

The boat stopped at the newly restored Reichstag, where its famous glass dome was beginning to take shape. A few passengers got off and the boat moved on towards the forbidding bulk of the cathedral, looming above the trees like some great beast. Built for Kaiser Wilhelm II, it had proved indestructible to wartime bombs, after which the communists, having no need for God, turned it into a museum. Now it crouched there, uncertain of its function.

They left the boat at Museum Island and walked across a bridge over daisy-filled lawns and on through a series of small streets and squares, once part of the Jewish quarter. A family of Russian violinists, the youngest around eight, were playing Bach with a virtuosity worthy of the concert hall, and a little further on an old zither player plucked out gypsy music for all he was worth to a group of dancing children.

It was a long walk to Pankow and they were already hungry, so halfway there they took a bus. In the restaurant, Gunter ordered blinis and caviar and they drank chilled vodka. The scent of flowers drifted in through an open window from a stall in the street and the restaurant was full of lively Russian talk and laughter. She could almost imagine they were in St Petersburg, which she'd never visited but always wanted to. At such a moment it was easy to forget the hatreds that refused to be laid to rest.

It was four o'clock when they left the restaurant and Gunter suggested coffee in one of the last of the old havens that remained in the rapidly changing heart of Mitte. She saw a tall, dilapidated house propped up on one side by wooden struts, a fragment of terrace that had survived the bombing. From the once magnificent hallway a wide staircase led to upper floors, with interconnecting rooms where people talked, reclined and were served tea, coffee or schnapps by elegant waiters wearing tight black trousers, white shirts and fancy waistcoats, who looked like flamenco dancers. The rooms were decorated in puce, purple or yellow ochre, darkened by age and smoke, with rattan chairs and stained divans piled high with velvet cushions that seemed to have come out of a Somerset Maugham story. On the first floor they played Vivaldi, on the second modern electronic music, and in the furthest room a woman was singing an operatic aria. At the top a somnolent quiet reigned and the air was thick with marijuana smoke. Eli went to the window and looked down into the overgrown garden where people were preparing a fire for the evening barbecue. It felt like being at some bohemian house party, where one knew none of the other guests.

They took a seat in a room on the second floor and ordered coffee. Eventually, drawn by the scents of roasting meat, they descended to the garden. It was growing dark and the trees were festooned with lights. Gunter ran into a couple of friends and they sat together under an ancient lime, balancing on their knees plates of lamb and couscous and drinking wheat beer. Eli, with her rapidly improving German, joined in the conversation, and she and the woman agreed to meet up the following day at a newly opened museum in Unter den Linden. A half moon appeared in the orangey darkness, and as she gazed into its brightness she thought how good it was to be alive.

A couple of days later they were having breakfast at the kitchen table. Gunter was preparing a list of locations for his producer and Eli reached for the newspaper. On the front page was a photograph of smashed tombs and overturned gravestones daubed with swastikas. The headline read, 'Jewish cemetery desecrated. Neo-Nazis suspected'. The caretaker of the cemetery was quoted as saying that the attack hadn't been discovered until the morning because the previous day was the Sabbath when the place was usually closed, and it was also a public holiday commemorating German unification.

'Have you seen this? A hundred and three graves smashed!'

'Let me see.'

Gunter reached for the paper. 'Jesus! Those scum never give up!' His voice was tight with anger.

'Their way of celebrating a unified Germany, apparently.'

'They're beneath contempt!'

'It says they've got fingerprints off some of the graves so maybe they'll be able to identify them.'

'If so they'll only be the foot soldiers.'

'That's a start.'

'What's needed is for the whole city to take to the streets. Force the police to actually do something. People won't face the fact that this kind of thing's the responsibility of each and every one of us.'

That evening Eli was in the bath and Gunter watching football on TV, when the phone rang. She caught snatches of conversation through the half open door.

'But that was three years ago. The police should have wiped his records by now… Christ! OK. I'll be there.'

She heard the click of the receiver being replaced and, wrapping a towel around her, got out of the bath.

Gunter was standing at the living room window, staring out into the dark. He turned as he heard her approach and she saw the faint rhythmic twitch at the corner of his mouth.

'What's happened?'

'That was Malgorzata.'

'Your ex-wife?'

He nodded, and she felt a sudden cold invade her.

'Bruno's being held at a police station in Charlottenburg. Since he's not yet eighteen, we should be allowed to bring him home, providing we guarantee his court appearance.'

The word 'we' seemed to exclude her as thoroughly as though suddenly she'd become a stranger.

'What's he done this time?'

Her tone was cold, though he didn't seem to notice.

'Marble like glass retains fingerprints. Apparently his were on one of the graves at the Jewish cemetery.'

'How do they know they're his?'

'A minor misdemeanour when he was fifteen. They should have destroyed the records but they didn't.'

'My God! Can it get any worse?'

He hardly seemed to hear her. 'I'll take him to his mother's. That's his official address. Of course I share responsibility for seeing he doesn't break whatever bail conditions they set.'

'You're going now?'

'I'm picking up Malgorzata on the way.'

'How's she taking it?'

He shrugged. 'You can imagine!'

She stood there getting cold, whilst he hunted around for things he might need for identification. Eventually she went into the bedroom to put on a dressing gown. If there'd been any point, she'd offer to go with him. But it was between him and his ex-wife now.

'Wake me when you get back if I'm asleep. It doesn't matter how late,' she managed to say.

He kissed her and was gone.

Restlessness kept her awake. A nasty incident with Bruno and his punk band had turned into a full-blown crisis. Gunter would have to spend whatever small amount of time he could spare from his work on trying to save his child from the clutches of the law, and prevent him from committing further outrages against Jews and God knows who else. She tried to imagine what could make a youth with all his advantages turn into a fascist. She was out of her depth and had no idea what to do.

It was getting light and she had only just fallen asleep still wearing her dressing gown, when she heard Gunter return. She listened to him clattering about in the kitchen and a few moments later he put his head round the door.

'You awake?' He sat down on the edge of the bed, looking exhausted.

Her head ached with sleeplessness. 'What happened?'

'We had to sign an affidavit promising to keep him under curfew until the trial. A sort of house arrest.' He sighed. 'He refuses to say anything. He went to bed as soon as we got him home. I stayed there for a while talking to Malgorzata. I don't think either of us knows what to do.'

She had never seen him so full of despair, and her heart softened. 'Come to bed.' She reached out a hand.

'Yes. If I can sleep for a couple of hours the day may not be a total write off.' He kissed her hand before releasing it. 'I'm so sorry! I can't believe I'm inflicting this shit on you.'

'Shit's the word!' She tried to make it sound light.

'The trouble is, it's me who's responsible!' He looked more dejected than ever.

'Come to bed,' she repeated.

In the morning Gunter left early and Eli went on sleeping, She was woken by the phone, and as she picked up the receiver her eyes fell on a note. It said he had gone to the office to collect some papers and would be back before lunch.

A woman's voice said, 'Gunter?'

She knew at once who it was. 'He's not here. Can I take a message?'

'Is that Eli? It's Malgorzata.'

'He's at the production office. He shouldn't be long if you want to call again.' She did her best to sound friendly.

'Thanks. I'll try him there.' There was brief pause then

she said, 'If he's already left, would it be all right if I came round to wait for him?'

Eli hesitated. 'If that's necessary.'

'Thanks. I'll be about twenty minutes.'

She got out of bed. She'd have to make herself decent for Gunter's ex-wife and there was barely time for a shower and a coffee. She felt herself being drawn deeper and deeper into a disaster that had nothing to do with her.

Fifteen minutes later the bell rang. She shoved her feet into some shoes and went to the door. She'd seen a photo of Malgorzata with Bruno amongst some family pictures in an album. In the flesh she looked different. She was a good-looking woman, though the fine skin around her eyes and mouth was criss-crossed with tiny lines and she appeared strained. They were physical opposites: Eli dark with Sephardic features inherited from her father and a tendency to voluptuousness, Malgorzata tall and lean with high cheekbones, slanting green eyes and short blonde hair.

Eli led the way into the living room and asked if she could get Malgorzata something to drink. Malgorzata said tea, and Eli disappeared into the kitchen. Despite an instinctive hostility towards Gunter's ex-wife, she felt a twinge of compassion for her obvious distress. She hoped Gunter wouldn't be long.

When she returned, Malgorzata was pacing up and down. 'I'm sorry to barge in on you like this. It's so hard to get hold of Gunter these days.'

'He's very busy with his film.'

'When isn't he! Still, none of this is your problem and I feel bad you've been dragged into it.'

Eli sat down and Malgorzata followed suit.

'The worst of it is, Gunter and I are responsible,' Malgorzata went on, changing to fluent English.

'I can't believe what a child does is ever entirely the parents' fault,' Eli said, doing her best to be conciliatory.

'Maybe. But I, at least, should have seen this coming. Gunter hates confrontation, and with his son worst of all. His mother was a very judgemental woman. A high-minded Protestant of the old Prussian school, good at making people feel guilty and ashamed. You never really escape that kind of upbringing.'

'You mean he should have been a stricter father?'

'No. He should have got to know his son better.'

'From what I understand he did his best. Bruno hasn't been turning up when he's supposed to.'

'A bit late in the day.'

Eli said nothing. This woman had spent half her adult life with a man she'd known barely a year.

'Bruno's disappeared,' Malgorzata announced.

'My God! When?' For a horrible moment Eli had a vision of him turning up at the flat.

'During the night. I wanted to tell Gunter face to face because I know how badly he will react.'

'When did you miss him?'

'I went into his room this morning and he was gone. Last night he went to bed before Gunter left.'

'D'you know where he might be?'

'With his friends, I presume.' She shook her head. 'He was such a delightful child. He hated school and any kind of authority but he wasn't rebellious. That's not unusual. I hated it myself.'

'What will you do now?'

'I don't know. That's why I'm here.'

Footsteps pounded up the stairs and a moment later Gunter burst into the room. He was angrier than Eli had ever seen him. He slammed his fist down on the low table with such force the mugs leapt in the air and made the women jump.

'That young idiot! Just let me get hold of him. I'll kill the little fucker!'

'You have to find him first. How do you propose to do that?'

Malgorzata's cool tone had the effect of a dose of cold water. Eli observed them as if they were two people in a play.

'I'll start by going down to the police station and reporting him missing. At least that'll save you the trouble.'

'That might be a good idea.'

'Jesus, Malgorzata! What's happening here?' The statement came out as a kind of moan. 'God, the next thing we'll hear he's put a bomb in some asylum seekers' shelter!'

He paced to the window as if the room were too confining. 'Tell me. Is this my fault?'

'He's not a child any more. He knows what he's doing. I have to go. I'm late for work.'

She turned to Eli. 'I enjoyed meeting you. In other circumstances I feel we could be friends.'

Eli bid her goodbye. She felt neither warmth nor hostility towards this woman into whose proximity chance had thrown her.

Gunter went to a cupboard, took out a vodka bottle and glass, and poured himself a drink. He took a swig then turned to Eli.

'Sorry! I wasn't thinking. D'you want one?'

She shook her head.

For the next few days they pretended to go about their lives as usual, though they both jumped whenever the phone rang. Gunter spent most of his day at the production office, and Eli decided it was a good moment to visit Munich and see what she could find out about Erich Klossowski, who'd worked there as a set designer in Max Reinhardt's theatre company.

It was raining when she arrived in Munich but the clouds soon passed and gave way to a pleasant day. The city was beautiful and compared to Berlin remained firmly connected to its pre-war past. Instead of bulldozers and bombsites, there were elegant squares and shops selling national costume – dirndl skirts and embroidered blouses for women, lederhosen and tyrolean hats for men. The cafés displayed mouth-watering cakes and pastries and sounds of a zither drifted out into the street, reminiscent of *The Third Man* – though of course that was Vienna.

The Pinakothek Museum had a magnificent collection of paintings, and among the photographs in its archive section several of the Reinhardt theatre company, taken during and just after the Great War. She found nothing that showed the young Balthus or even his father, Erich. So, disappointed, she made a few photocopies and left the museum. She'd planned to find a bierkeller or bistro for dinner and spend the night in an inexpensive hotel. But as she walked through streets and squares where the cafés were filling up with prosperous-looking people, some in national costume, suddenly all she could think of was getting back to the rough reality of Berlin, and Gunter. She made her way to the station, caught the next train and arrived there some time after midnight.

The flat was in darkness and she assumed he must be asleep. She put down her bag and went quietly into the bedroom. The bed was empty but there was a light under the kitchen door. He was slumped at the table in front of a half-empty bottle of vodka. He looked up blearily and her anger burst forth. She'd cut short her visit to Munich and hurried back to the place she was supposed to call home, only to find him in a state of drunken self-pity.

'Is there any food?' she snapped.

She hadn't eaten since lunch.

'Sorry! I wasn't expecting you.' He made a visible effort not to slur his words.

'Obviously!'

She went to the fridge and rummaged through the tired-looking vegetables and bits of cheese mouldering there. He observed her in silence as she put together a sandwich and brought it to the table.

'There's a lot more about this situation you don't know,'

'Now isn't the time to tell me.'

But he was not to be put off. 'I need to. But if I do I'm afraid it will change your feelings.'

'Shouldn't I be the judge of that?'

'Yes.'

She remained silent. Let him talk if he would. It made little difference.

'I painted a rather rosy picture of Bruno's childhood. I wish it had all been like that.'

His eyelids closed and for a moment she thought he was falling asleep. She ate her sandwich and waited.

Eventually he said, 'D'you want me to go on?'

'You've started so you might as well.'

'When Bruno was ten, the film I was about to start got cancelled and my work suddenly dried up. Malgorzata decided to get a full-time job to pay the bills.'

He got up and poured himself a glass of water. Talking seemed to sober him up.

'Being a house-husband was harder than I'd thought. I began spending the hours when Bruno was at school in bars and cafés, drinking and smoking dope, with the occasional

125

fuck to take my mind off the mess I was in. If she knew, Malgorzata chose to ignore it.

'One particularly black day when I'd been trying to write but had mostly been drinking, Bruno came home from school and refused to eat the food I'd made for him. I ordered him to stop complaining and get on with it and he shouted back that he hated me and my filthy food and threw it on the floor. I yelled back, demanding to know if he'd any idea what it was like being stuck there in that apartment day after day. He looked at me with his cool gaze that reminded me of my mother and said, "It's your own fault you're a failure."'

He emptied his water glass.

'I pulled him up from the table, shoved his arms into his coat, saying I'd show his smug little arse what real failures were like, and marched him out of the house. We got to my usual bar, where people who thought it bohemian to be slumming it amongst other no-hopers hung out. No doubt they made me feel better about myself. To a child the place must have been horrific!

'I remember very little about the rest of the evening. I'm told I was hauled into a taxi hours later by a couple of mates slightly less plastered than me and that the barman called Malgorzata, who picked up Bruno.'

'What did you do then?'

'Once I sobered up I was too ashamed to go home. I returned a couple of days later. Malgorzata was icy but more reasonable than I could have imagined. I tried to explain something of the madness I'd descended into but she didn't want to hear. She told me if I wanted to talk to someone I'd better see a therapist, and I did. I stopped drinking and got a job at a TV station. The hardest thing was rebuilding a relationship with Bruno. For years I've worked at it and in the end I thought I'd succeeded.'

'And thinking about all this is why you got drunk tonight?'

He grimaced. 'Bruno has contempt for weakness. To him compassion is a form of weakness.'

'And Nazis are strong and Jews are weak for not having defended themselves under Hitler. That's how his thug pals think too, no doubt.'

'Something like that.'

'So what does Bruno with all his advantages have to do with them?'

He put his head in his hands. But she was in no mood to be sympathetic.

'If you ask me the incident you describe wouldn't be enough to turn someone into a Nazi. Children are resilient.'

'Then why?'

His question resounded in the semi-darkness.

Berlin, 1922
Balthus

In Berlin the Prime Minister, Walther Rathenau, had been assassinated and the French were threatening to occupy the Ruhr and part of the Rhineland. In response to the escalating economic crisis, cries rang out on all sides for retribution against the plundering of the homeland. Merline found the German language, which had already become abhorrent to René, infected with xenophobia to the point where she too began to hate it on her tongue. Once she had argued with René that one couldn't equate a whole culture with the corrosive politics of the times, citing all the childhood tales they'd loved, the philosophers and poets that made up their rich cultural heritage. Now even the music seemed tainted by the corruption and despair into which society had fallen.

Anti-Semitism was also on the rise, as yet not so much against ordinary people as those wealthy Jews, owners of successful businesses who lived in the big houses along the lakes. Balthus listened to the adults debating how it wouldn't be long, given the mounting hysteria, for them all to become scapegoats. His grandfather, the old cantor from Breslau, had recently joined the family in Berlin, making the overcrowding even worse. His mother loved her father, and welcomed his presence whatever the inconvenience. His patience and good humour had shielded her, the youngest child, from the critical exigencies of a mother who always favoured her son over her daughters. But to Balthus he was a stranger, and his childish jokes and alien beliefs only increased his irritation.

Most evenings Balthus returned home late from school when the family had already eaten supper. He told Merline he'd walked to save on the U-Bahn fare and she knew it was futile to question him further. He was almost fifteen, tall as a grown man, and his striking good looks made him a ready target for predators. He no longer shared with her the thoughts and passions of his remarkable imagination, and she understood his reluctance to return to the noisy chaos he was supposed to call home without even a bed of his own to sleep in.

One evening as he made his way back to the apartment he saw a group of youths striding towards him along the street. There were about a dozen of them, swaggering and chanting as they went so that other passers-by were forced to step into the road to avoid them. At first he didn't catch what they were saying, but as they drew nearer he made out their words, 'Knallt ab den Walther Rathenau, die gottverdammte Judensau!' 'Do for Walter Rathenau, that goddam Jewish pig!' The deed was already done but the words sent a chill into his bones. The mood of fear, added to the daily deprivations, was making life in this city increasingly unbearable.

Already in Geneva his response to an existence without comradeship had been to turn inwards, to create his own secret world where hurt pride and censored thoughts could be forgotten. He lived for René's letters, and whenever he received one he read and reread it, refusing to share its contents with his mother. School held no importance for him since none of his teachers were the least interested in the subjects they taught, or cared about anything other than where their next meal or drink were coming from.

For Merline he was like a young sapling struggling towards the light. She wondered if he even remembered the long Geneva afternoons when sun filtered in through the trees outside their window throwing patterns of warm colour onto the floor. They'd dreamed together of how it would be when they returned to Paris, but these days he'd become a stranger. One evening he came home wearing a pair of smart cowboy boots and when she asked where he'd got them, he said he'd bartered them for a drawing. She didn't believe him and in desperation wrote to René asking him to send whatever money he could so that she might get Balthus back to Switzerland, if necessary alone. She felt less and less able to protect him from the disaster she sensed was lying in wait.

But despite the city's threatening atmosphere, its chaotic decadence also fascinated Balthus. Things that had once revolted him, now aroused a perverse excitement. Walking the streets after dark, he was drawn to the lights of the crowded clubs and bars, where sounds of laughter and jazz issued forth whenever a door opened or closed. After the dreary hours of school or the stifling intimacies of the family apartment he longed for such conviviality. He took to hanging around the entrances to breathe in smells of alcohol and tobacco.

The hectic sexuality of people hell bent on pleasure called to his adolescent fantasies, and the desire to step inside one of those brightly lit interiors and experience it for himself was becoming more and more pressing.

He began to save the pennies given him each day to buy food and train tickets until he would have enough for a couple of beers. The place he chose for his initial visit was in a district on the far side of town that had developed a reputation for nightlife and where he ran little danger of being recognised. It was more of a club than a bar with a security guard at the door, who wore leather gloves and a heavy overcoat. He looked the young man up and down before deciding his money was as good as anyone else's and waving him in.

It was still too early for the place to have got going and his first impression was disappointment. If he had expected a den of iniquity full of dangerously glamorous people, he found a clientele that looked shabbily ordinary. But as he gazed around him, he picked out a few fashionably dressed women accompanied by men whose gold teeth and sharp suits no doubt made up for bald heads and protruding bellies. He bought a beer, found a small table next to a noisy group of young men and sat down.

After a while one of the young men got up and paused in passing at his table. He pinched his cheek with a teasing smile then laughed and moved on. Balthus observed him in the mirror above the bar as he ordered drinks and flirted with the barman. His movements were graceful and he was clearly aware of his good looks. For the first time it occurred to him the power bestowed by youth and beauty and he felt a stirring of excitement.

For the next couple of hours he made himself inconspicuous and observed the scene. Once or twice he had to look away when accidentally he made eye contact with someone, but no one bothered him. The young men at the next table got up and left. More people arrived as the place filled and grew noisy. He amused himself by watching the dancers and noticing how people, as they became drunker, grew more uninhibited and sometimes belligerent. The mottled hand of an old man at the next table roved across the thigh of a girl young enough to be his granddaughter, a bejewelled dowager clung to a bored chaperone half her age who petulantly refused to dance. Eventually he grew bored and decided to leave.

It wasn't easy to explain his lateness or the beer on his breath and he knew his mother didn't believe him when he told her a schoolmate had given him wine pastels. He didn't care. This life without privacy or refinement, lived in sordid proximity with people he felt nothing in common with, disgusted him. Only with René had he ever experienced the communion he longed for, and now that was threatened by his mother's unreasonable demands. There were times when he hated her for her intensity and the dramas she made out of the simplest thing. But there were others when feelings of love and compassion almost choked him. He longed to escape to Paris like his brother Pierre, whose footsteps he dreamed of following in as soon as possible.

On his next visit to the club, the doorman recognised him and greeted him with a conspiratorial nod. As soon as he entered, he spotted the group of young men he'd noticed before. They waved him over to their table as old friends. Pleased to be part of such lively company, he sat down. They were dressed even more flamboyantly, and he noticed several of them were wearing makeup. It was clear from their loud laughter and outrageous manners they were intent on attracting attention, and after the initial greetings they soon forgot about him. He listened for a while to their brittle conversation. It was hard to believe that people who looked so remarkable should in reality be so mundane. Eventually he made an excuse, got up and left.

He took up position, leaning against a wall near the dance floor. His gaze settled on a girl dancing by herself. She was very skinny with small breasts half visible through the embroidered muslin of her dress. Her gaze was dreamy and unfocused as she swayed to the music. He watched her until the number came to an end. She left the dance floor and returned to a table where a well-dressed man wearing spats and a pinstriped suit was seated with two women in fancy toques and brightly coloured silk shifts that clung to their ample breasts and thighs.

The man started to pour wine into the girl's glass, but she covered it with her hand and instead took the cigarette one of the women passed her. She inhaled deeply, sucking in her cheeks. After a few seconds she burst out in a fit of coughing. The others laughed and someone slapped her on the back. The band struck up again and she got up to dance, reaching for the man's hand. He refused but instead of sitting down, she turned, sashayed boldly over to where Balthus was standing and planted herself in front of him with a provocative smile.

He knew it was risky but he allowed her to pull him onto the dance floor. His only experience of dancing was capering wildly round the living room with his mother. This manoeuvre turned out to require scarcely more skill. The girl draped her arms around his neck and pressed her thin, bird-like body against his as they clung together, barely moving. Held in her sphinx-like gaze, he knew she must feel his erection but that only enhanced his excitement. Once he glanced over his shoulder and caught the eye of the pinstriped man. The sense of danger added to his thrill.

Suddenly he found himself pushed roughly aside as the girl was pulled off the dance floor and he watched the two women gather up their bags and boas from their chairs and push her out in front of them as they made for the exit. The pinstriped man followed without a glance in his direction. But someone came up behind him and whispered in his ear that he'd better watch his step if he knew what was good for him. When he looked back after the girl, she was gone.

With nothing better to do, he wandered over to the bar to order another beer, before realising he'd run out of money.

He dared not ask the stony-faced barman for credit and risk the humiliation of a refusal. An elegantly dressed woman seated at a nearby table who'd been observing him, reached out and grabbed his sleeve. He turned to meet her blue gaze and noticed the scar that ran down her face from eyebrow to chin in a thin raised line.

'Don't go, pretty Jew boy! Stay and have a drink with me.'

He looked down at the imprints of her long red nails in the flesh of his wrist and as he caught her aroma of perfume mixed with sweat, his stomach clenched in nausea. He wrenched his arm free and made a dash for the exit.

As he ran through the streets the seductive purr of her voice echoed in his head, repeating over and over the detested phrase, 'Don't go, pretty Jew boy! Pretty Jew boy!'

Switzerland, 1922
Balthus, Merline and Rilke

Pierre had already left for Paris when Balthus arrived in Beatenberg. His mother had promised him he'd never again have to return to Berlin, but he had little faith in her ability to keep her word. In the hush of the Swiss countryside, though he'd hated the conditions in which they'd lived, he recalled the hectic life of crowded city streets with a kind of nostalgia and felt more isolated than ever. René was the one constant in his life and he clung to the hope that he'd fulfil his promise to get him to Paris after his sixteenth birthday. René was a genius who remained true to his art in the face of every obstacle, and he, Balthus, would prove himself a worthy protégé.

When Merline arrived in Beatenberg she was shocked to see how tall and thin he'd grown in the short time since she'd last seen him. His lanky frame seemed hardly to support him and her heart clenched with love as she took in the fledgling down on his sharp-featured face and the hair falling almost to his shoulders, half-hiding his wolfish grey eyes. Six months ago she would have taken him in her arms without a thought. Now, fearing a rebuff, she refrained.

She observed the single-minded way he worked when making a drawing or constructing a puppet for the theatrical dramas he still occasionally entertained them with, but she knew less and less what went on inside him. It was her own fault. She and René were the only people he was close to, apart from his brother. Yet how often had she boarded him out to be alone with her lover. It was hardly surprising that all he wanted from her now was to help him get to Paris.

From René no longed-for invitation to visit Muzot arrived, but instead a letter:

Steel yourself now to the love, whatever its name, which can grant me my life... For if I were to give up all that is mine, and, as I often long to do, fall blindly into your arms and lose myself in them, then you would be holding one who has sacrificed himself; not me, not me... I cannot dissemble, and cannot change myself... I kneel in the world and implore forbearance from those who love me. May they spare me! Not use me up for their own happiness, but help me to the unfolding of that solitary happiness but for whose great signs they would not have loved me.

It was as if he were addressing his faithful public rather than writing to her, his lover, though in his eyes such honesty was no doubt evidence of how much he still valued their friendship. It was also proof her demands had become as irksome as all the others that daily besieged him. The truth was the passion that was her raison d'être had only ever been for him a transitory source of inspiration. Now he needed to complete his latest cycle of poems, and he had done with love.

But as René withdrew from her, his relationship with Balthus strengthened daily, giving the boy new feelings of importance. He was now the chief point of contact between his mother and her erstwhile lover, and with no fear of emotional entanglement René willingly shared with him his thoughts and ideas. Balthus made little attempt to hide his triumph, and Merline did her best to hide her resentment. He would remain for her the son for whom she would make any sacrifice that he might fulfil the great promise of his remarkable talent.

She made a sketch of him as he worked, imbuing it with all the feeling she was capable of, and sent it to René. He wrote back by return, showering it in praises:

… delicious, of an incomparable tenderness and melancholy charm. The most beautiful and harmonious thing you've accomplished in my view!

'*Yes!*' she replied, '*The child is marvellous. Braver and more grown up than I am, for instance.*'

Even so slight a reference to her jealousy would not pass him by, but why should she resist the least expression of the feelings that for the most part she did her best to suppress?

Erich Klossowski was also in Switzerland and came to visit them in their apartment. Despite the years of separation, he still liked to play husband when they were together, making his presence for Merline nearly unbearable. She remained tied to him both legally and for the small financial help he was occasionally able to provide. Balthus, though he loved and admired his father, seemed little more at ease with him.

As soon as Erich had gone, Merline wrote to Rilke:

I had a visit from my friend for ten days and as always that tired me and made me nervously exhausted. I believe that with time it will become insupportable. I fear more and more a life together. This morning at seven the guest left. I began to put

everything frenetically in order as if I was sweeping out the
devil... Yesterday before going to bed, my friend made me a
present of the Abbé Julio's 'Blessed at Notre Dame'. I placed
it between my breasts and it scratched me badly so I observed
that the Abbé Julio found himself somewhat embarrassed in this
position and we began to laugh. Once he'd been well warmed up,
I put him on my night table. The result: my day, though without
hope, was sweet and sun-filled.

The disingenuous note of flirtation on which she ended the
letter was designed to provoke, as René understood well. He
knew how she longed to cut the ties that bound her to Erich,
but her uncertain existence and his own inability to offer any
alternative made that impossible. What made the situation
even more poignant was that it was to him rather than to
Erich the boys looked to secure them a future.

He sent Balthus a copy of Dante, from which he refused
henceforth to be parted. But still there was no invitation for
Merline for a more prolonged visit to Muzot. She dreamed
of it, sleeping and waking, real as a mirage. Without Muzot
and without René she had no future in Switzerland. The only
hope was to follow her sons to Paris. In her old studio, with
the things she'd left behind as hostage to her eventual return,
she might reclaim some of the independence she'd lost. But
getting there wouldn't be easy. She was in trouble with the
Swiss police for failing to surrender her German passport on
arrival, and without passport or visa she was at the mercy of

the French consul. At night she lay in bed going over and over what must be done, and praying for a word from René that would make it unnecessary.

For René, Merline had become a burden on both his conscience and his heart. Of all the demands he daily received, hers were the hardest to satisfy and his strength was all but used up. At times he was so tired he could scarcely get up from his chair. His doctor had suggested a sanatorium, and Merline was in Beatenberg waiting for his invitation. All he could think of was that he must conserve his dwindling strength for his work and that meant being alone at Muzot. And yet he owed her so much.

He wrote to his closest friend, Nanny Wunderly, whom, he believed, above all his other friends had his true interests at heart. The previous summer he had written to her:

After such a prolonged period of productivity, I am ready to have Merline at Muzot again for a stay during the summer months. She so desperately needs a break from Berlin and has written to you, I know, to ask whether you might have need of her services for a while. I am as ever grateful to you for all your efforts on her behalf but her health is not good from all the stresses she is forced to endure and I do not forget how much it is to her efforts that I owe this small kingdom of mine.

This year, drained of compassion by weariness and ill health, he wrote:

M. is one of those people who, having once received a payment at some counter, keep coming back to it even when the official assures them nothing has come in under their name.

Nanny Wunderly wrote back at once, making no attempt to conceal her satisfaction that at last he'd come to his senses on the subject of Merline. She urged him on no account to relent. But a few days later, despite her admonishment, he could no longer hold out and sent Merline an invitation to join him.

She arrived, humble with joy and gratitude and determined not to be a burden. She moved into her old quarters at the top of the tower, and spent the first day watching the light that filtered in through the arched window of her room as it changed from hour to hour. The following morning she dressed and walked through the early mist to the nearby farm for vegetables, eggs, and a chat with the farmer's wife. They sat outside in the yard and drank bitter black coffee with plenty of sugar from china bowls to the soothing clucking of hens and noisy interruptions from the farmer's wife's pet goose.

After breakfast she worked in the garden whilst René went on sleeping. The warm summer air, intoxicating with the scent of the roses she'd planted the year before, was thick with the drone of bees and life teemed around her. Each day had its rhythm. In the morning she busied herself with tasks and in the afternoon made drawings or simply gazed out at the landscape until the light faded. In the evening after they had eaten they read together or talked with their old companionable ease. It was enough to live in the moment in this place that meant so much to both of them, not thinking of what was to come. What did the hostility of others matter as long as René welcomed the care and love she offered?

At the end of August they went to visit Balthus who'd been left behind in Beatenberg. He told René how much younger and prettier his mother was looking. But despite his cheerful words, René saw the air of loneliness that surrounded the boy. He, too, had had his childhood stolen from him, with lasting consequence. But it was in that place imagination took root, and as he looked at all the marvellous things Balthus had produced, he showered him with heartfelt praise. The boy's ability to wrest knowledge from the most unpromising conditions and to put it to creative use would, he knew, be his salvation. Like his mother he was a true artist, but in his case he would let nothing stand in his way.

Berlin, 1994
Eli

Eli paused to consult her street map then turned into a quiet tree-lined street off one of the main boulevards in Charlottenburg. She was on her way to see Malgorzata, her excuse to return the papers Gunter had needed to sign in relation to Bruno's police investigation.

Malgorzata lived in an old building that had survived the war, with solidly handsome balconies on each floor and at the back a courtyard enclosed on three sides. Hers was the top of the list of names next to the entrance. Eli pressed the bell, and as the buzzer went pushed open the heavy door.

As in Gunter's building there was no lift, only a wide staircase leading up from a tiled hallway, and by the time she was nearing the top she was out of breath. She glanced up and saw a young man gazing down on her from the landing above. With a shock she recognised Bruno.

'Hello! Is Malgorzata at home?' she said in German.

'No. Was she expecting you?'

His manner was cool but not hostile.

'I left a message on the answer phone. D'you know when she'll be back?'

She was doing her best not to sound breathless after her climb. He shrugged his shoulders.

'You can come in and wait if you like.'

He was barefoot and dressed in jeans but she easily recognised the capering figure she'd seen on the lorry, manically plying his guitar. With his slight build and timid gaze that slid away from eye contact he looked like any youthful boy, not in the least her idea of a fascist.

'You are Eli? You live with my dad, I think,' he said in heavily accented English, as he led the way into the flat.

'Yes.'

'You know I must stay in this apartment. How do you call it? House arrest!'

He grinned as if it were amusing.

'I heard you'd gone missing.'

'Well, I'm back now… Do you want tea? My mother does not drink coffee.'

'Tea'll be fine, thanks.'

The kitchen was off the entrance lobby, with space for a small table next to the window, which looked out onto the courtyard and a line of sentinel-like poplars as tall as the house. The neighbourhood had an air of genteel prosperity, very different from Kreuzberg.

He offered her a range of green and herbal teas.

'How long before the trial?' she asked.

'About a month. I am lucky. In your country I would be in a Young Offenders' Remand House, I think. Not so pleasant!'

'I guess it's not supposed to be pleasant!'

'I have friends in England. The British and Germans have a lot in common.'

She suppressed a wry smile at the solemnity of his pronouncement.

'How long have you lived in this apartment?'

'All my life. We shared it with my grandparents. My grandfather looked after me while my parents worked.'

The mention of grandparents was news. Gunter had given her the impression Bruno had been entirely his responsibility.

She waited to see if he'd say more, but he didn't so she turned the conversation to his band.

'We have been invited to play at a festival in Holland. Bands will be coming from all over Europe, including Great Britain. Now I will not be able to go.' He paused then added theatrically, 'Music is my life!'

She had the sense he was playing a part for her benefit.

'Do you think your mother will be home soon?'

'I don't know. You can wait for her, if you like.'

'I'd better go.'

'OK. I will tell her you came.'

She fished a large brown envelope out of her bag and laid it on the table.

'Can you make sure she gets this? It's from your father.'

'Sure!' he said, barely glancing at the envelope.

She stood up. 'Thanks for the tea.'

He got up too, ducking his head politely and standing so erect that for a moment she almost expected him to click his bare heels together.

As he held open the front door for her to pass through, she thought he might give her some message for his father but he said nothing. Halfway down the stairs she glanced up and saw him leaning over the banister. It made her think of a lonely child she'd once seen, watching his parent leave.

On the way home she made a diversion through Tiergarten to get her thoughts in order before returning to the flat.

Seeing Bruno in the flesh made her more aware than ever how little she knew about Gunter and his life before her. Hers by comparison was like a blank sheet of paper on which even Simon and the abortion scarcely registered. Bruno struck her as a fantasist rather than a hardcore thug. The grandfather he'd mentioned might well be invented since it was hard to imagine an extended family crowded into that small flat. Gunter most likely withheld information because he didn't consider it important. But now that had changed and there was a pressing need for openness. She completed a lap of the park and turned for home.

When she got to the flat, he was preparing supper and wonderful smells issued from the kitchen.

'It's going to be a special meal to show you how happy I am you're here. I'm sorry for being too preoccupied to show you that.'

In a sudden burst of affection, she went over and put her arms around him.

'And I'm happy to be here with you!'

He kissed her.

'So let's celebrate by devouring this fine fish I've prepared. Followed by some passionate lovemaking!'

They ate the fish until only the bones remained, after which she felt so full she suggested a stroll before bed.

Down by the canal the sounds of the city gave way to the lapping of water and the wind in the trees. She lengthened her stride to keep pace with his. Eventually she said, 'I took the papers back to Malgorzata today. You never said grandparents lived with you. It must have been crowded in that small flat.'

'Did she tell you that?'

'No. In fact she was out. Bruno was there.'

'Bruno! He's back? Why didn't you say?'

'I didn't want to spoil your lovely dinner.'

'Christ! How come she didn't call me?'

'Maybe she didn't know. I think he just came back before I arrived.'

'The little bastard! Sorry! You're the last person I should take my frustration out on.'

She hesitated. 'The grandparents he mentioned, were they Malgorzata's parents or yours?'

'Hers…'

Across the dark water of the canal two swans were moving sedately as if propelled by some unseen force.

'It can't have been easy having them both living with you.'

'It was useful for babysitting. She was a nice woman. He, on the other hand…'

'You didn't like him?'

'You could say that.' He paused. 'He was a right wing Ukrainian nationalist who'd willingly collaborated with the Nazis. God knows how many innocent people died because of the information he handed over about the movement of Allied troops and supply routes.'

'What happened to him after the war?'

'He escaped trial mainly because he'd seen to it no one was left alive to testify against him.'

'How did you find out?'

'He wasn't ashamed of what he'd done. He considered himself a German patriot, a war hero. He hated the Soviet Union, and often declared his belief that the Germans might be beaten but one day they'd rise again to take up their rightful place in the world.'

'And you let him look after your son?'

He sighed. 'He loved the boy. By then the war was long over and Bruno knew nothing of those things.'

'How did Malgorzata feel about him?'

'As a child she saw very little of him. He travelled round the country selling farm machinery.'

'And her mother?'

'She was Polish and quite different. Whenever he heard the two of them speaking Polish together he insisted Malgorzata confine herself to speaking correct German. The photographs of her mother when she was young show a beautiful woman. But by the time I met her she was old and incapable of taking even the smallest decision, like what to cook for dinner. She'd started to drink, secretly at first but when he refused to give her money she began selling things from their apartment until it was virtually bare. It was obvious she couldn't manage when he was away so Malgorzata brought her to us.'

'This was before Bruno was born?'

'Shortly after. Bruno's birth gave her a new lease of life. She even managed to stop drinking. We in turn were only too grateful for the babysitting. Hours at a time she sat with the child in her arms, singing songs she remembered from her childhood. You never saw such a contented baby.'

'I know how important grandparents can be. So what happened to them?'

'She died when Bruno was two, of a stroke. He survived on his own for a while, but since for years he'd avoided paying tax or national insurance he had only a meagre pension. Then the government cancelled compensation to foreign war veterans so he had virtually nothing. Malgorzata agreed he could stay with us as a temporary measure and for her sake I went along with it. In her culture it's the child's duty to look after their parents no matter what they're like.'

'That must have been tough.'

'Surprisingly it wasn't bad. He could be charming enough when he wanted and he kept his opinions to himself. We were both working so we saw little of him. Bruno was only five and not yet at school. It was useful having him there.'

'And Bruno loved him?'

'Adored him, and he devoted himself to the child. He took him to cinema and ball games, told him tales about brave Slavic heroes full of blood and revenge. By the time we got home, Bruno was usually in bed, begging his grandpa for one last story.'

'You weren't worried about his influence?'

'All that worried me was the film I was making, and his being there made that possible. What I see now is that for Bruno his grandfather was the one person who was there for him.'

He fell silent.

'How long did this go on for?'

'He died of a heart attack when Bruno was nine. Malgorzata and I felt little but relief. For Bruno the loss was huge and neither of us paid sufficient attention. My next film collapsed and she had to work longer hours to make up the money, so I replaced the old man as child carer. A poor substitute in Bruno's eyes.'

Down by the canal the light from the street lamps scarcely penetrated the thick foliage and the only sounds were their footsteps and the water.

'Have you talked to Bruno about these things?'

'I've tried but he cuts me off. He says his memories are his and nothing to do with me.'

He reached for her hand.

'I guess it's too late to change things.'

Geneva, 1924
Balthus

Balthus was to leave Switzerland after his sixteenth birthday celebrations at the end of February and to follow in his brother's footsteps to Paris. René wrote to him regularly from

Muzot, informing him of negotiations with Gide about the financial assistance he was offering and giving advice on what to do on arrival. The arrangements were in René's hands now and Merline was aware how little she had to contribute. In her eyes sixteen was too young to be let loose in a strange city, especially someone like Balthus, indifferent to danger. But she kept her fears to herself.

She wrote to René:

When I objected very timidly to Balthus that he might lose himself in Paris, he simply laughed. He has had his hair cut and wears it brushed back. So there, chéri, you are a grandfather and I have a grown up son!

He was at the station to meet me, a bit pale and melancholy since there has been no further news about his departure. At the house I admired the work that he had done. He is a great, great artist… a prodigy and no one here sees it.

It is six o'clock and the tailor who lives across from me is playing his clarinet. Today looking at Balthus' paintings, I said to myself that perhaps this is only an interregnum and with these gifts something is going to happen, that I must not despair. But so much is necessary at fifteen years old to become a great painter. You see, darling, I don't lack courage. On the contrary I am a little overwhelmed by so many promises of happiness.

Despite his mask of indifference his mother's anxieties undermined Balthus' confidence, which he masked under a guise of impatience. Whenever he received a letter from René he hid it from her, knowing how she would seize on it for any glancing reference to herself. It was his revenge and he was proud that he, not she, was now the principal recipient of René's correspondence. His mother continued to regard him as a child, but René treated him as a friend and equal in ways she could never be to him.

Under René's tutelage he had come to look on both his parents with a more critical eye. His father's opinions were disappointingly conventional, and his pronouncements on art, despite his erudition, uninspiring and academic. Unlike René he showed little interest in what Balthus was actually doing or thinking and, though quick to make judgements, rarely offered encouragement.

His mother, on the other hand, had always been his loving companion, opening his eyes to the beauties of the world and tirelessly inventing things to amuse and engage his imagination. It wasn't entirely her fault if he found her love suffocating and her childish enthusiasms irritating. What irked him most was that she continued to focus her life on René, despite the fact it was clear they were no longer lovers, and unaware of the contempt she brought upon herself and her family by her claims on him. Most intolerable of all was when she railed at some reported slight from one of René's influential patronesses, going so far as to insist the grand lady's objections were on account of her race. He recalled furiously how when money was short she'd proposed taking the three of them to live with René's close friend, Nanny Wunderly, where she would take on the role of housekeeper and he and his brother would be companions to the children. The three of them would be little better than servants, all the proof such people needed that such was the rightful place for the semi-educated daughter of a cantor from Breslau and her offspring. It made her claims to be part of Muzot absurd, yet she failed utterly to see it.

Paris, 1924
Merline and Balthus

March 7th 1924, Beatenberg

My dear René,

Balthus this morning left for Paris. I had decided to finish with this useless waiting, above all as I had received a letter from Gide which enchanted me and persuaded me it would be a good thing if Balthus left.

For myself, I must remain here a little while longer. If a few days with Pierre in Paris proves impossible, I shall try to make a rendezvous with Gide. I regret having used up all my resources in Switzerland. It would be very useful now to be able to sell one or two pictures. The French consul has been very obliging, though, and sent me as I asked him the passport express for the day of my departure. It is with a mixture of excitement and

*sadness, which you will all too readily understand, that I now
feel able to contemplate a future.*

*Your loving friend,
Merline.*

If she had any other choice involving René she would have
seized it, but she had not. At least by following her sons to Paris,
she could preserve for a little longer a semblance of family life
and oversee Balthus' studies. There was no money for him
to be enrolled at art school so an alternative programme of
study had to be devised. Nothing was insuperable as long as
she never had to return to Germany. If necessary she would
make her way to France without papers.

She left Switzerland at the beginning of March, abandoning
any remaining difficulties with Swiss bureaucracy to René. She
was returning to her old apartment at 15 Rue Malebranche
near the Jardin du Luxembourg, which throughout the terrible
Berlin years had remained perfectly preserved in her memory,
a beacon for some unimaginable future. As she crossed the
border into France only the need to preserve some dignity
prevented her from falling to her knees and kissing the ground
beneath her feet.

Paris looked battered and grey in the aftermath of the war.
Several familiar landmarks had disappeared, but despite the

trauma the city's soul had not been destroyed and would revive as it always had. After a grim winter the Luxembourg Gardens were full of tender green and the sound of birdsong. Children played on the swings and in the sandpits watched over by uniformed nursemaids, lovers sauntered arm in arm or lingered on benches, and now and then the almost forgotten sound of human laughter floated on the air. She walked slowly along sandy paths between neat rows of budding flowers, raising her face to the spring sun and breathing in the scent of wood smoke that mingled with the still sharp breeze. Bit by bit the numbing anxiety that for so long had dogged her was sliding away, like the shedding of an outworn coat.

Each day as soon as she woke she went to the window and looked out over the familiar landscape of rooftops and sky, thanking God for her deliverance. When she went into the streets to buy food or take a walk through the neighbourhood, she noted with relief how beneath the shabbiness little had changed. The red-cheeked man and his wife from the country, grey-haired and somewhat shrunken now, continued to run the greengrocer's shop on the corner, and the butcher she'd frequented had been joined by his youngest son. Both wore black armbands, and one day he confided to her that his two oldest boys had been lost in the war. Only the local café was unrecognisable, run now by strangers, Italians, who seemed harassed and unfriendly. Most of the day she spent in her studio, relishing the hours of uninterrupted concentration and the rediscovery of skills she'd feared lost.

Balthus too was in his element, his spirits undimmed even by having to share an apartment with his mother. Parisians, whatever their deprivations, wore their hardships lightly and with style, and after years of frustration he felt life opening up. Most days he went to the Louvre to make copies of selected works, which René had recommended as the best way for an artist to gain an education. Unlike Germany, art here wasn't merely the reflection of the grossness of daily life. As he walked through museums and galleries filled with unimaginable treasures, he searched for some continuity between the infinite riches of the past and this ravaged present. Though eager for experiment and new perspectives, the prevailing modernism did little to stir his imagination and made it all the more necessary to find a style of his own.

In the evenings he walked the boulevards or sat over a beer in a café, breathing in the distinctive smells of dark tobacco and sweet odour of coconut oil mixed with jasmine some of the women wore. Their appreciative looks made him conscious of his own attractiveness, without the threat of danger that existed in Berlin. He was making new friends, members of the art and theatre scenes that were rapidly re-establishing themselves. He shared none of this with his mother, mistrusting his ability to contain her eagerness.

Often she woke to hear him returning late into the night but wisely said nothing, confident that at least here he would come to no harm. Gradually she was reconnecting with some of the old friends and acquaintances who'd survived the upheavals of the war, and a few weeks after her arrival received a note from the painter Bonnard. Rilke had informed him that she and her sons had returned to Paris and suggested he might visit her at her studio. She replied at once they'd be delighted to receive him for tea the following Thursday. What most excited her was the prospect of introducing him to Balthus and showing him his work.

She ran to answer the doorbell and there stood Bonnard, tall and slightly awkward with his courteous, old-fashioned greeting. Recognising his shyness put her more at ease and she reached out her hand to welcome him. He was as uncomfortable with small talk as she was and as soon as he entered the living room turned to examining the watercolours that decorated the walls, commenting and praising each of them, one by one.

Eventually she interrupted him. 'My son, monsieur, is the real artist in the family,' and called to Balthus to fetch the drawings he'd been working on.

To give the two of them a moment alone together, she excused herself and ran down to the patisserie around the corner to buy cakes for tea. As she entered the shop, she saw amongst the cornucopia of tarts and pastries some of her old favourites, delicate pastry shells filled with pistachio crème-pâtissière and decorated with a lick of dark chocolate. She chose three, plus three strawberry tarts, and waited impatiently whilst the elderly serveuse placed them carefully into a pink cardboard box and tied it with string.

When she returned, the cups and saucers had been pushed aside and Bonnard was examining Balthus' drawings that were spread out over the table. He looked up as she entered the room.

'Madame, you are absolutely right! The young man has exceptional talent!'

'And never a formal painting lesson in his life!' she replied.

Balthus removed the drawings and Merline undid the cake box. She placed them one by one onto a plate, rearranged the table for tea, and invited them to sit down.

'M. Rilke recommended making copies in the Louvre as the most useful preparation for becoming an artist,' Balthus declared.

'Indeed! I too profited greatly from the practice as a young student,' Merline responded eagerly. 'Each day I took my stool, drawing pad and satchel to the Louvre or the Grand Palais. The problem was whether or not to keep my hat on since the other artists, almost all of them men, dressed so informally. In the end I took it off and hid it beneath my stool.'

Bonnard joined in her laughter and Balthus got up to fetch the kettle from the kitchen. Her prattle infuriated him. She was surely boring the great man to death. But when he returned Bonnard was still smiling, and seemed quite charmed by his mother. His mouth full, he related several stories of his own struggles with tutors, whom he declared either antiquated academics or fervent young modernists who pronounced representational painting dead. Balthus crumbled his pastry between his fingers and longed for the visit to be over.

When at length not a crumb of cake or drop of tea remained, Bonnard wiped the remains from his beard with the dainty napkin Merline had provided and screwed it into a ball. He looked around as if uncertain what to do with it, until she reached forward and gently took it from him. He stood up, thanked them both for a delightful afternoon and declared he really must be going.

At the doorway he kissed Merline's hand, thanking her again with obvious sincerity for the most delightful afternoon. Then he turned to Balthus.

'Young man, I've a friend who owns a gallery in the Rue Royale. If he agrees, I will set up an introduction for you to show him your work.'

Before Balthus could reply, Merline interjected. 'That is so generous and thoughtful of you, M. Bonnard! We should be delighted, wouldn't we, Balthus?'

'Not at all, dear Madame! It is what the young man deserves. He's a real artist... I look forward to our next meeting.'

And with a short bow he was gone.

Merline turned to Balthus, eyes shining. But his expression was dark.

'How could you, Maman! You made us seem like beggars and fools!'

She placed her hands on his shoulders, her pride undaunted.

'We have nothing to be ashamed of, my son. You heard what M. Bonnard said. "He's a real artist!" What greater proof do you need?'

With the money René was able to provide for Balthus and what Pierre earned as secretary to Gide, which also entailed a place to live, Merline was at last freed of some of her anxieties. She saw Pierre whenever he had a free day, and hoped he was happy with his lot. She knew he wouldn't say if he wasn't, out of concern for her. The last time they'd met he spoke enthusiastically about Gide's latest novel, a chapter of which he'd given him to read. His shyness often made him appear overly serious, even a little dull. But she knew him to be intelligent and thoughtful, and by far the gentler of her two sons.

About Balthus she had no such worries. He'd taken to the city like a duck to water and was rarely at home. He'd long since ceased to confide in her, and took every opportunity to assert his independence. He was becoming increasingly concerned with his appearance, and she wondered if he'd acquired a girlfriend, though he gave no hint of it. Often he came home with some new item of clothing or piece of fine fabric he'd picked up at the flea market for a song, and asked her to make it into a waistcoat or scarf. She resisted questioning him, and when he donned the finished garment with barely a thank you, she remarked to herself with what fashionable flair he wore his clothes.

To him she said, 'You're becoming quite the dandy. I've seen the admiring looks you get!'

'I enjoy choosing my own things, if that's what you mean. After all those hand-me-downs,' he snapped in retort.

It was hard to find the right tone with him these days. She knew her chatter drove him from the house, yet silence felt unnatural. But the pleasure of having the studio to herself and the luxury of being able to concentrate on her work were compensation for his absence.

A few weeks after their arrival in Paris, she received a letter from René saying that he'd persuaded a German industrialist friend to pay a yearly stipend to each of her sons in order to continue their education. She wrote back at once, thanking him once more for his generosity and unfailing commitment to her boys:

> *They will each write to you separately, and I feel sure prove themselves worthy of your faith... But now, René, there is something else. I must beg forgiveness for the terrible recriminations I have heaped on you from Berlin. I pray that your understanding may allow you to see my complaints for what they were, not your fault but the mark of my desperation. After all to whom else could I have expressed the longings of which only you knew the reason and the cause?*

René wrote back by return:

> *I destroyed the letters on reading them, because I knew they did not come from the hand of she whose courage has never abandoned her, even in the face of the worst adversity.*

I have always believed that one day, in spite of all you have endured, you would recover your capacity for joy. Your life might be solitary now, but for the first time you are living it as you yourself have chosen. Surely that is the greatest of blessings?

'It is true,' she replied. *'And the chief cause of those blessings has been your enduring support and affection.'*

Her belief in the undying nature of love remained her raison d'être. But still she could not deny the tone of formality that had replaced the intimacy with which once they'd their expressed their thoughts and feelings.

Recognising a new confidence in her tone, René wrote again a couple of weeks later announcing his imminent arrival in Paris. Before she had time to reply there was a ring at her door and there he was, holding in his hand a bunch of blue gentians. She cried out in delight, burying her face in the flowers and welcoming him in. As she hurried to put them in water he watched her go, once more the woman whose rare capacity for spontaneity had drawn him to her in the first place and that he'd feared gone forever.

The last of his reserve melted as she told him excitedly over tea how well the boys were doing, and that she herself was working and sleeping better than she had in years. She asked what he was writing, and he replied it was a sequence of poems that would probably be his last. She scoffed at such a notion. But in moments when he lost his animation she observed the unhealthy pallor of his skin and puffiness around his protuberant blue eyes. He had an air of exhaustion, but when she asked about the visit he'd recently made to a sanatorium he refused to talk about it, stating merely that they'd found nothing wrong. It did little to put her mind at rest.

They met almost daily, falling into a pleasant rhythm of walks, exhibitions and dining with friends. The fine weather held and colour returned to René's cheeks. Each day seemed like a blessing, though instinct warned her such times might not be repeated. His presence in Paris had become known and a wider circle was opening up to her than the few friends she'd been reacquainted with. It was a milieu that without him would have been beyond her reach and, whilst she savoured each occasion, she knew few of these people would maintain contact with her after he was gone. Not everyone was pleased about the resumption of her relationship with Rilke, and snatches of gossip reached her that he'd once more fallen victim to La Klossowska. She did her best to feign indifference. Let them say what they liked. She asked nothing from him other than the affection he seemed so ready to give, and she knew her presence did him nothing but good.

By August they were discussing a trip to Italy, and began to make plans. They would go via Burgundy, then Muzot, and on to Milan. Merline grew increasingly excited, above all at the thought of seeing Muzot and her beloved garden again. René's willingness to receive her there was a sign of the great trust he still placed in her, and she would do nothing to threaten it.

They left Paris at the end of the month, stopping first at a small hotel beside the Lago Maggiore. He seemed tired by the journey but insisted there was nothing amiss. On the second evening, just before dinner, he complained of stomach pains and suddenly became violently sick. Merline got him into bed and called for a doctor. It was clear that however much he denied it, his health had been deteriorating for some time and it was impossible not to be alarmed.

The doctor examined him and pronounced food poisoning. To René she appeared relieved, but she did not believe the diagnosis. The doctor's authoritative manner couldn't hide the fact that, like the experts before him, he had no idea what was wrong. And though René accepted his assertion that there was nothing serious, she could see he was afraid.

They stayed on at the hotel and she did her best to reassure and divert him, hoping for an improvement. They had their meals brought to the room and most of the time he spent in bed, sleeping as much as his discomfort allowed. When he felt a little better he got up and went to the window, gazing out at the surrounding mountains whose threatening magnificence seemed to her more claustrophobic than picturesque. He spoke little and she could only imagine the thoughts that preoccupied him. He left the room only to go down the corridor to the bathroom, and the few morsels he ate he had difficulty in keeping down. It was obvious the planned voyage was out of the question, and she had little difficulty in persuading him to cancel Milan and to go with her instead to Sierre.

She took rooms for them at the Hotel Bellevue, where they planned to stay until he was well enough to decide where he wanted to go next. It was a difficult journey, but once settled into that small, friendly inn where he felt at home, he revived. They talked of the time not so long ago when they had passed days of delirious happiness there, and the memory brought comfort.

It was now late summer. In the still warm days, filled with the scent of flowers and buzz of insects, he gradually gained strength. In the mornings, seated at his bedside, she read to him or drew whilst he went on sleeping. Sometimes they read to each other from his latest work, and these were the moments she treasured most. As his strength returned they began to venture out in the afternoon, walking arm in arm along the lane where blackberries were ripening in the hedgerows and through the woods where leaves turned yellow and russet. In the evening when it grew chilly they watched the mist rise up until it filled the valley, and Merline felt a peace rarely experienced throughout her turbulent life. Bitterness dissolved and the wound caused by her exile from Muzot was healing. She understood such contentment was transitory, that the bleakness of separation would follow and the memory of this quiet joy would not be sufficient to combat the darkness to come. But for now it was enough.

As the days shortened into October and the nights drew in, René grew increasingly restless to return home and resume work. Merline was forced to acknowledge that as soon as he could travel, she must see him back to Muzot and return to Paris. She offered to stay with him as housekeeper and, as expected, he refused. Even his dread of being alone was not enough for him to agree to such an arrangement. The only thing she could do for him was to secure the return of Frieda, the one person he seemed able to tolerate.

Invigorated by the prospect of returning home, René accompanied her to the station for the Paris train.

'Oh, René! How many times have we done this, and on how many countless station platforms?'

She leaned towards him from the open window and he reached for her hands. He kissed the fingertips and, when he looked up, she saw his eyes filled with tears and it was all she could do to maintain her mask of calm.

'D'you remember when you said that it was me who gave you back the power to write, which you believed gone forever? Nothing will ever mean so much to me!'

A shadow of pain passed over his face, and she smiled to soften the impact of her words. She knew too well he was not made for passion or permanence and what meant so much to her merely drained him, especially now when he must conserve his dwindling strength.

As the train pulled out of the station she watched his figure grow ever smaller until it disappeared altogether. She closed the window and returned to her seat, choking down an intolerable grief. As the rhythmic chant of the train bore her swiftly on, she knew with sickening certitude that this was the last time they would ever meet.

From Paris she wrote to him:

Oh, René, how small you became, and how unreachable. My heart is overwhelmed.

She received no reply. She was not surprised. He was preparing for a winter of work, during which his copious letter writing must be put aside. But the terror of foreboding would not leave her:

Has nothing bad happened between us? Tell me that it is still good. Are you so ill that all love for me stands still?

For a week she heard nothing until finally on her birthday she received a telegram. The message was strangely formal and did nothing to put her mind at rest. He must be very ill, or perhaps one of his rich patronesses had taken charge of him, blocking further communication. Unable to keep silent she wrote back, begging him to tell her what was wrong and if she might make a brief visit to him.

More weeks of silent heartache went by, during which she could neither work nor think. At last on December 23rd she received his reply. It was as distant as the previous telegram, and as she read and reread the few words printed there her body tensed in fear:

If your loving heart were to counsel you to come, you would be ill advised. Your journey would be useless since no one is permitted to visit me.

In a trance she prepared the Christmas meal for the sake of her children. Afterwards they walked together in the Jardin du Luxembourg to see the fireworks. A huge Christmas tree was decorated with golden angels sounding their trumpets to the night sky, and crystal snowflakes glinting in the light of a thousand candles. Pierre took her arm but Balthus remained aloof, as if he too felt the shadow of approaching doom. All evening he'd made no mention of René, and she dared not ask whether he'd received his usual Christmas message.

When it was time to return home he announced he was off to celebrate with friends. Pierre accompanied her to her door before returning to his lodgings. Alone, she relit the candles on the tree and sat drinking the wine left over from dinner and watching them slowly burn down until the room was left in darkness.

Five days passed, a time of fear and numbness. Then on December 29th she received the telegram she'd dreaded. It said that at midnight on the 28th René had slipped into a coma and died of the leukaemia that had gone so long undiagnosed. Slowly, as the words gathered sense, she felt as if she'd been struck a physical blow that left her gasping. The world collapsed into a chaos of meaningless fragments, sounds of a tap dripping in the sink, the creaking of a pipe, or a fly buzzing against a windowpane. After a few hours confined within her four walls, she found it impossible to breathe. She put on her coat and walked the streets, until cold and damp drove her home again. Pierre came to see her. He made tea and sat holding her hand without speaking. But Balthus, unable to bear his mother's grief, absented himself, seeking comfort from the company of friends. Only once, the night after the telegram, long after she was in bed he came into her room and asked if she was all right. She didn't blame him. He too was grief stricken, and what was there to say?

On January 2nd, a cold, bright winter's day, René was buried in his beloved Valais. In Paris the weather remained grey. Merline walked the length of the quays, along the left bank of the river, across the bridge, and back down the other side. She reached home after dark, exhausted and barely conscious. Balthus had gone to the funeral, but she was not invited.

Part Two

Berlin, 1995
Eli

The bedroom window in Gunter's flat looked out through trees onto the canal. Eli's desk was in front of it, with her books, papers and laptop. She was trying to find out what happened to Merline after Rilke's death, in an effort to complete her story. But there were no more letters, records ceased, and her voice fell silent. It was like a bereavement.

She laid out all the material she'd collected, books, photos, photocopies of documents and transcripts made from library books that had to be returned, in a kind of mourning ritual. She felt keenly the injustice of Merline not being invited to Rilke's funeral. Those who'd considered themselves guardians of his legacy had always done their best to nullify her importance in the great poet's life, and they'd succeeded. She, who'd sacrificed herself on the altar of love, had been reduced to a mere footnote in his biography.

Perhaps, living quietly in her old Paris studio, she'd managed to rediscover herself as a painter. But then came the Second World War and the German invasion of 1940. She'd done too much running to leave at the first opportunity. But as life for Jews got more dangerous and Balthus fled to Savoy and then in 1942 to Switzerland, she might have joined him there. Pierre, who at least had her interests at heart, would probably have persuaded her. The only fact Eli was certain of was that he had been with Merline when she died in Paris more than twenty years later, and that Balthus was not present.

Eli had read somewhere a quote from Rilke that all he'd known since childhood was 'the dungeons in the castle of love'. The love that was Merline's raison d'être, to him was merely imprisoning and degrading. And like his mentor, Balthus too had done his best to shake off former intimacies, especially with his mother. No doubt in his child's eyes she had betrayed him when she chose René. But he'd had his victory, replacing her as René's closest confidante, the one with whom René shared the intimate passion of his imagination.

The previous day she'd come across a photo of Balthus with Artaud, taken in Paris in the early 1930s when he'd collaborated on a production for Artaud's Theatre of Cruelty. It was remarkable how alike the two young men were, tall and slender with fine, aristocratic features and a cultivated air of disdain; two perverse elitists she could easily imagine flirting with the fascist views currently gathering force in Europe. Rilke had expressed admiration for Mussolini in his final years. He wrote that he considered him the perfect antidote for what he called that 'excess of liberty that is the world's disease'. In the chaos of economic collapse, he believed Mussolini to be the person best placed to re-enforce order 'with the right modicum of violence'. And Balthus, with an unshakeable belief in his own superiority engendered by all the lavish praises of his boyhood, found being a poor, stateless Polish Jew intolerable. He deeply resented the lack of those privileges that should rightfully be his, and spent the rest of his life fighting to reclaim them.

Modern fascists were of course very different from those of the 1920s and 1930s. For one thing, they cared little for art or culture. Yet they too felt threatened by those they held to be inferiors, foreign interlopers mainly, bent on robbing them of their inheritance. It was a disease that hadn't gone away.

A letter from home reminded Eli that the following Saturday was Rosh Hashanah, Jewish New Year, and one of the few religious festivals her family observed. It offered a new beginning, something she felt she and Gunter badly needed. Since Bruno's arrest, though they rarely spoke of him, his presence hovered over them like a pall. From time to time Gunter would regain his natural optimism. But his good mood seldom lasted.

To mark the New Year she decided to cook a special dinner and invite a couple of his close friends. Afterwards they could go dancing. But when the day arrived, she could see he was in no mood for company and settled on dinner at home for the two of them. She scoured the neighbourhood for marrow bones to make osso buco, his favourite dish, decorated the table with flowers and seven candles in a silver menorah she'd picked up in a junk shop, and waited for him to return from the production office.

Touched by the surprise she'd so carefully prepared, he kissed her affectionately and asked what was the occasion. She told him it was Jewish New Year and, as important, the anniversary of their moving in together. He opened a bottle of Rioja and made a toast to a brighter future.

'It's not rituals themselves I object to,' he said. 'It's the claims of those who practise them to be in sole possession of the truth. The same with politics. They all share the conviction that the end justifies the means.'

'Which is why my parents rejected religion.'

'And mine embraced communism. At the time it seemed the antidote to fascism.'

She set down a steaming dish of osso buco.

'One religion exchanged for another!'

She ladled food onto his plate then served herself.

'That smells good!... It's not just communists. It's the RAF, the lot of them.'

'The RAF?'

He laughed.

'No, my love, not your gallant British airmen! What the Baader-Meinhof became…' He took a bite of his food. 'Mmmm! Tastes wonderful too!'

'Were you involved with those people?'

'No, but my girlfriend was.'

They concentrated for a moment on eating. But her curiosity was aroused.

'Those people, the RAF? Weren't they terrorists?'

'Most would call them that.'

'So in what way was your girlfriend involved?'

'It's a long story.'

'We've got all evening.'

'Why spoil this lovely dinner?'

'When we've finished I'll bring in the cheese and then you can tell me.'

She changed the plates, put a dish of cheese and grapes on the table, refilled their glasses, and looked at him expectantly. She was not going to let him escape.

'I'd sensed for a while that Jana, my girlfriend, was getting involved with things I'd rather not know too much about. It became more serious when a woman friend of hers, a big bossy type I didn't care for, told me she had to disappear for a while.'

'So what did you do? You'd no idea this was going on?'

'We were all political then but not in an organised way. More a rejection of all authority.'

'But what drew her to such people?'

'Like Malgorzata's her family were refugees, but Jana's family were much poorer. Her mother was Russian, unable to read or write. Unlike Malgorzata she dropped out of school and went to work in a shop. She was intelligent, a free spirit but frustrated by lack of opportunity. It was what attracted me to her, apart from her beauty. She taught herself to type and got a job as an admissions secretary in a local hospital, which she hated. Most of the radicals she mixed with were from privileged backgrounds, with all the knowledge and sophistication she coveted. They welcomed her as a natural recruit, and I guess that made her susceptible.'

'And you think that justified what she did?'

'I'm not saying that. I'm trying to answer your question. She wanted change and like most of us knew it would never come by traditional means. She didn't plant bombs or kill anyone, and I guess she didn't realise that as a mere mule working in the supply chain she was expendable once her cover was blown.'

'So what's the difference between those people and the ones Bruno's involved with? Both use murder as a weapon, only one lot are right-wing extremists and the other so-called left!'

'There are differences.'

'You mean the fact that one side claims to believe in equality and workers' rights?'

She was hot with righteousness, fuelled by jealousy of this Mata Hari whose claims on Gunter seemed even now to outweigh her own.

'You have to understand, Eli, it was state violence in '67 that gave rise to the student protest movement. When the students demonstrated against the Shah of Persia's official visit to Germany, his personal guard shot at them like it was sport. Even when they killed a guy the police just stood by and did nothing. We realised then we were still living in a police state.'

'What about Malgorzata? Was she part of all this?'

'She wanted even less to do with politics than me, though we sympathised with the students.'

'So what happened after Jana disappeared?'

'I'd been to the Alps for a few days and came back to Berlin. The place must have been watched because no sooner had I switched on the light and put down my bag when four armed policemen burst in, smashing the door off its hinges. They were in full riot gear, protection shields held out in front of them. They shouted at me to lie face down on the floor and handcuffed me. Then one of them put his foot in my back and started firing questions. Where was Jana, how long had I been a member of the RAF, and so on. I told them I knew nothing, but they went on shouting and pointing their weapons for another hour or so. It would have been farcical if it hadn't been so frightening. My arms had gone numb from the handcuffs and my body was aching all over, but still they wouldn't let me up and went on throwing out names and accusations, none of which I knew anything about. Finally they told me to get up and they were taking me to the station to make a statement. They bundled me into a van and I was let out several hours later and told to report back every week. I was to let them know the moment I heard from Jana or any of her friends and needn't think about setting up any secret meetings because I'd be watched at all times. As I was leaving the police station I noticed Jana's picture had been added to the gallery of wanted terrorists on the wall. That meant it would be posted up in every railway station and airport in the country. It was the first time I felt really afraid for her.'

'And you never saw her again?'

'Some years ago in London I was coming out of a cinema and I recognised her. She was ahead of me in the crowd with a man. They set off up the street together and I ran after them, calling her name but she didn't turn round. When I caught up with them, I confronted her. She looked me in the eye and said matter-of-factly, "I'm not Jana. My name is Leah." Then she turned and walked away... That was a long time ago. You were still a teenager.'

Yes, she thought, a naïve young fool, oblivious of politics and what was happening in Europe. Not until the demonstrations against Thatcher's poll tax had she begun to wake up when she went with some friends from school on a protest march in London. Gunter, on the other hand, had lived with the consequences of fascism and catastrophic defeat in this benighted city, doing what he could to confront them. However questionable his actions, he'd been in the thick of things, and not for the first time she asked herself what he saw in someone as ignorant and opinionated as herself.

'I never think about these things now, except you asked me,' he said gently.

Bruno's trial was fixed for October 18th. Gunter and Malgorzata would both be there but neither was to be called as witness. Gunter had his hair cut and sent his only suit to the cleaners. He even borrowed a tie from someone at the production office. Eli told him what a handsome figure he made, whom anyone would be proud to call father. There were still a couple of hours to go before the trial, but his restlessness made it impossible for him to settle so he decided to walk to the court. She wished him luck and kissed him goodbye.

Once he had gone, she washed up the breakfast things and set about cleaning the flat. When there were no more chores she could think of, she decided to go for a walk. Whatever the outcome of the trial, at least it would put an end to uncertainty and they could get on with their lives. She wasn't proud of the petulant way she sometimes behaved. But love made one selfish. She remembered Merline suggesting to René she might send Balthus to live with her sister in order to be with him, finding too irksome the presence of her beloved son. And Gunter, whose chief love was his work, admitted that as long as he believed his child to be well cared for, he'd happily abandoned him to others. Was that all love was, the pursuit of one's own desires at the ruthless expense of those you were also supposed to care for?

Gunter had agreed to call her as soon as the proceedings were over and loaned her his work mobile phone in case she wasn't home. She decided for a change to go to Schloss Charlottenburg and take a walk through the park. The day was bright with barely any wind and the sun felt warm, though it would get chilly as soon as it went down. The leaves of the trees were vivid yellow against a perfect blue sky, and smells of damp earth mingled with the mild stench of stagnant water from the canal that fed into the lake. The flowerbeds in front of the chateau had already been cleared for winter, leaving only bare soil and a few boxed shrubs, and as it was a weekday there were few people. The place felt forlorn, as if powerless to preserve its antique glory in the face of the bulldozers and cranes bent on erasing the past.

When she got back to the car park, the café was still open. She went in, ordered a glühwein and sat down to wait for Gunter's call. She was sipping the hot, comforting liquid when the mobile rang.

'Gunter?'

'He's got a year's detention, though he could be out in a few months. The judge said he had to make an example of him to show other young people the activities of far right organisations won't be tolerated.'

His voice sounded faint as if he was somewhere where he had to speak quietly.

'How did he take it?'

'The judge asked if he had anything to say but he refused to speak. The prosecution concentrated on the attack on the Jewish cemetery. When they took him away, he didn't even look at us.'

'Come home, darling.'

She could hear voices of people coming and going in the background.

'I'm going for a quick drink with Malgorzata first. As you can imagine, she's very upset. I'll be back as soon as I can.'

'I'll be waiting.'

Her heart was heavy. This wasn't her fight, but as long as she was with Gunter she was part of it just as inextricably as if it was.

In early December she received a phone call from her editor in London.

'How's the article coming along?'

'Michael!' Her heart leapt at the sound of his voice, as if coming from another world. 'Slowly. Things here have been a bit chaotic.'

'I'm calling because Balthus will be in Paris in the New Year. He's agreed to an interview but my back's playing up again. I told him how well informed you are and passionate about his work. He's agreed you can go in my place.'

She could hardly take in what he was saying.

'Really? That's wonderful! But you're sure he's OK with it?'

She recalled all too vividly their previous encounter at the Grand Palais, and it was unlikely he'd forgotten it. She couldn't risk a second humiliation.

'Have you something more important to do?'

Michael seemed irritated at her lack of enthusiasm.

'No! Of course not.'

'He's an old man. You won't get another chance.'

Gunter congratulated her when she told him and said it was testament to the esteem in which she was held at the magazine. Also, it was good timing since he himself would shortly be leaving for Africa. When they returned, they'd both have something to celebrate.

Each week Gunter was allowed a visit to the Young Offenders' Institute, which he kept to religiously despite the fact that sometimes Bruno refused to see him. He was determined to show his love and support for his son no matter what he'd done, and understood, he said, that Bruno's refusal to see him was one of the only self-determining choices he had in that place. Eli kept her opinions to herself. She spent the days up to Christmas writing and rewriting lists of questions designed to catch Balthus off guard and push him into giving more than his routine performance.

The city shut down for Weihnachten. Shops and offices closed, the streets emptied and people retired to the bosom of their families. There was a rather dismal celebration at the Young Offenders' Institute that Gunter attended, and after that he and Eli stayed home. Alone together, time ceased, the world slipped away and with it, its problems. It was as though they'd shed layers of uncomfortable clothes and returned to the simple joys of nakedness. They cooked goose and red cabbage and afterwards, tipsy and replete, lay on the sofa in each other's arms, admiring the crystal snowflakes sparkling in the light of the Christmas tree candles and the tree that smelt of the pine forest. They took it in turns to read aloud from Rilke's *Duino Elegies* and Eli thought how beautiful the German language sounded on Gunter's tongue.

In the bedroom she stood for a moment, naked at the window, gazing out at the frosty sky. She raised her arms to the moon in a gesture of pure delight.

'Come, my lovely girl!' Gunter said from the bed, holding out his arms.

She turned to face him, a silvery nymph caught in the moonlight, and entered his embrace.

At Silvester they went dancing, and even relentless grey skies could not destroy the harmony. But soon the holiday would be over. It was a good time to be going to Paris.

Paris, February 1996
Eli

The magazine had agreed to pay her fare plus two nights in a hotel. If she wanted to stay longer that was up to her. She took the train, even though the journey took twice as long, and checked into a small family run hotel on the far side of the hill in Montmartre. The area wasn't so touristy at this time of year and since there was an international fashion fair that week, all the hotels she knew were full.

After Berlin the city seemed filled with light. In the morning she walked in cold sunshine down the steep lane from Sacré-Cœur to the Rue des Martyrs, whose smoky bars and small shops offered a cornucopia of delights from fine food to African masks and rare stamp collections. The place had the look of one of Atget's photographs. Through a narrow doorway to a courtyard, artisans could still be seen working their trade, and children played on weedy cobbles, chasing in and out of washing hung there to dry. She thought of Merline walking these streets, joyful in the knowledge she would never return to the city she hated.

She entered a café, ordered a tartine and a large crème and took a final look at her plan for the interview. She wasn't due at the George V where it was to take place until 4pm. And, knowing what store Balthus set by appearances, aimed to return to her hotel beforehand to change into something less casual. Unable to concentrate, she finished her coffee, paid, and set off in search of a gallery in Opéra, where rarely seen paintings by Soutine were on show.

Opéra was full of tourists and expensive shops and the gallery was a tasteful conversion of a spacious town house. In the context of its cool spaces, Soutine's feverish, off kilter landscapes and still lives of bloody carcasses seemed aggressively out of place, as if threatening to burst out from their frames. He and Balthus were more or less contemporaries, yet the vivid colours and violent emotions of these paintings offered a striking contrast to Balthus' reined-in canvases, full of dreams and unexpressed desires. She wondered if they'd known each other's work, and if so what they'd made of it.

At three-fifty she entered the George V. It was like no other hotel she had ever been in. She watched as two uniformed flunkies conducted a pair of distinguished-looking guests down the wide corridor that led away from the reception lobby, guarded at intervals by huge vases of exotic blooms. A silk Chinese carpet partially covered its inlaid marble floor and on one panelled wall a tapestry depicted a scene of Fragonard-like revellers. The place breathed elegance and money, a fitting context for someone of self-professed noble lineage who'd done his best to expunge from all records the privations of his youth.

She gave her name to the receptionist, who greeted her with practised charm.

'I'm here to interview Count Klossowski,' she announced in a voice that seemed suddenly too loud.

'Your name, please?' the receptionist asked in heavily accented English.

'Elinor Kay. I'm from *Art Today*.'

The receptionist reached for a leather folder lying on the desk, from which she produced a note with Eli's name handwritten on a cream vellum envelope.

'This is for you.'

She handed Eli the envelope with a crisp smile and turned her attention to the large American waiting impatiently on her other side.

Moving away from the desk, she tore open the envelope. The handwriting was firm though a little scratchy where here and there the nib had stuttered on the paper's thick grain. It read:

Dear Miss Kay

I regret having to cancel our meeting today, to which I have looked forward. I have a dinner engagement this evening, which I fear would not leave us sufficient time to talk and which will require considerable energy on my part, something that at my age is not as inexhaustible as it once was. Perhaps we can arrange another time for our interview.

With all good wishes
Count Balthazar Klossowski de Rola.

She slipped the note into her pocket and found her way to the exit doors. Once out on the street she began to walk with little thought of where she was headed. The feeling of disappointment was crushing. Meeting Balthus had been the fulfilment of a dream harboured ever since she discovered his paintings at college. Not only was the chance to interview him in person the most exciting challenge of her professional life, it also offered the possibility of finding some resolution to the story of the Klossowskis.

How naïve she'd been not to realise the impossibility of relying on someone well known for being as manipulative as he was elusive. It was clear he'd had no intention of being quizzed by some lowly reporter like herself but had agreed to their meeting merely on a whim, or perhaps to humour his old friend, Michael. How foolish to imagine such a coup would simply fall into her lap! She felt like one of those poor birds he painted at the mercy of his malign cat, and all she wanted now was to go back to the hotel and sleep.

It was dark when she woke. The alarm clock on the bedside table said eight o'clock. She'd slept for three hours, but rather than feeling refreshed she felt drained and listless. She lay staring at the ceiling for several minutes, wondering what to do next. There was a whole evening to get through and she'd eaten nothing since breakfast in the Rue des Martyrs. She decided to get up and look for a restaurant.

As she cleaned her teeth in the bathroom, she pondered how Michael would take her failure. Perhaps he wouldn't be surprised, assuming it was a gamble that hadn't paid off. On the other hand he might blame her for not refusing to take no for an answer and letting slip the chance of a lifetime. She'd already proved at their encounter in Paris that door-stepping tactics were not her forte, and if being a critic meant adopting the hunting techniques of a tabloid journalist it wasn't for her.

189

She'd abandoned the thought of becoming a real artist and made up her mind to write about the painters she admired instead. Now even that ambition seemed illusory.

She stepped out of the hotel and shivered at the chilly night. Her leather jacket was insufficient protection against the cold but she couldn't be bothered to go back for a sweater. At the top of the hill there was a small row of shops and a little further on a restaurant. Without bothering to read the menu posted up outside, she entered and ordered the set meal.

The food was nothing special and the unpretentious atmosphere suited her mood. She sat brooding about Merline and her readiness to sacrifice everything, including her talent, to love. At least that gave her existence purpose, whereas her own life lacked all direction, drifting aimlessly from one city to another without even a place she could call home. She had a vision of herself, alone in some anonymous city in a rented room, still waiting for that mysterious thing to which she would give herself wholeheartedly, until eventually she disappeared without a trace.

An accordion player arrived. She listened indifferently as some of the diners joined in with one or two well-known chansons. Then he put down his instrument and the proprietor emerged from behind the bar, followed by two young men and one of the waiters. The four of them faced one another in a tight circle and, with one hand cupped over the ear and the other resting on the next man's shoulder, they began to sing. She didn't recognise the language, though she overheard someone at the next table say it was Corsican. The music was full of minor chords and strange Arabic harmonies that made the hairs rise on the back of her neck. It spoke of yearning and vast lonely spaces, and as her mind disengaged she entered deeper and deeper into a vortex where only the voices existed, calling out their longing that had become hers. At length the singing ceased and in the silence that followed she felt empty as though washed clean. Thoughts that had preoccupied her evaporated, leaving only vacancy, an empty road towards an unknown future.

She came to slowly, as though waking from a trance, to the sound of clapping from the other diners. She waited until the last of them were leaving, then paid her bill and got up from the table. She felt light-headed, though she'd drunk barely two glasses of wine. The proprietor held open the door and bid her goodnight with an old-fashioned blessing that reminded her suddenly of her beloved grandfather.

Outside, the cold struck. Below, the city snored gently like a giant beast at rest. She raised her face to a sky full of stars, indifferent as diamonds, and felt the moorings that bound her to earth give way so that at any moment she might drift, weightless, up, up into the chilly night. Only the sound of her heels clacking on the pavement as she descended the hill to the hotel, recalled her to the solid nature of her existence.

In the morning she awoke feeling calm, but with the same feeling of insubstantiality. She was in no hurry to get up so reached for the article she'd been intending to read in preparation for the interview that now would never take place. It was a spirited refutation by Sabine Rewald of the libel charges Balthus had brought against her for her introduction to the catalogue of his New York exhibition. In it Rewald wrote of a child he and his Japanese wife had given birth to, dead at the age of two of Tay-Sachs disease. The sickness that brought such tragedy was something, according to Rewald, that afflicted only male Ashkenazi Jews from Eastern Europe, and there was no record of its existence amongst the Japanese. The article also mentioned a breakdown he'd suffered in 1934 and a suicide attempt from an overdose of laudanum.

For the first time she asked herself whether pain, not pride, had driven him to reinvent himself. The urgent need to free oneself from the bondage of the past was a survival mechanism in the face of the hardship and upheavals of childhood that could take no account of who might be hurt in the process.

The bedside telephone rang. Assuming it would be Gunter, she reached eagerly for the receiver. The voice at the other end was that of a cultivated elderly man.

'Hallo? Is that Elinor Kay? This is Count Balthasar Klossowski de Rola speaking.'

She pulled herself upright.

'Yes, it's Elinor.'

'I hope you did not waste the rest of your day. Cancelling

our interview yesterday was a necessary inconvenience, I'm afraid, for which I apologise.'

His English was lightly accented and almost too correct. He paused, waiting for her to say something.

'I understand, though it was disappointing.'

'In that case, if you have time, would you care to meet today?'

She hesitated. 'When were you thinking of?'

'This morning, if that suits you. About eleven? I have to be somewhere for lunch.'

'What time is it now?'

'I believe it is nine-thirty.'

She would have to hurry.

'OK. I'll be there at eleven.'

'Good. Ask at reception and someone will show you to my suite.'

There was a click at the other end of the line. She replaced her receiver, feeling strangely calm. A quick bath to prepare herself for the encounter with this most slippery of tricksters would give a moment to think up a strategy. But as she lay there, breathing in the lavender oil she'd bought in some Aladdin's cave on the Isle St Louis, she decided it was better to leave things to chance. She got out of the bath and dressed quickly in whatever came to hand.

It was a fine winter's day. After a short bus ride, she walked the rest of the way to the George V. Low winter sun bounced off the river, throwing patterns of light onto the walls of adjacent buildings. Near one of the bridges a trio of Africans were playing music from Senegal, so infectious she began to dance. Catching her eye, the singer beckoned to her with wild, comic gestures that drew the attention of passers-by. When the song ended people clapped and threw money at her feet, thinking she was part of the troupe. She scooped up the handful of coins and tipped them into an instrument case that lay open on the pavement. As she turned to go, the singer called out to ask what she was doing that evening. She waved her hand in a gesture of farewell and hurried on.

She arrived at the hotel at ten past eleven and was shown to a suite on the second floor by a uniformed flunkey wearing white gloves. He walked ahead of her in silence along a wide corridor guarded by oversized bouquets of exotic flowers, until at length he stopped, knocked at a door, opened it and stood aside. It occurred to her she should tip him, but whilst she fumbled in her bag for some change he was already walking back the way he had come.

The room was large with three floor-to-ceiling windows that overlooked the garden. Light filtered through half-drawn blinds, throwing a soft glow over creamy yellow walls and carpet. There was a sofa and two easy chairs upholstered in pale pistachio velvet, and on a side table a bowl of cream roses beside a photograph in a silver frame of Balthus' beautiful wife and daughter. Between two of the windows was a walnut writing desk and above it a still life of fruit and flowers painted in the style of the Dutch masters. Everything had been chosen to create a soothing impression of elegance and good taste.

The door to the adjacent room opened and with a shock she recognised Balthus. In the flesh he looked both frailer and more vivid than she'd expected. He wore a dark blue velvet morning jacket and well-cut grey trousers, perfectly tailored to fit his tall, lean frame. A cream cashmere roll-neck partially hid his wrinkly neck, the only part of his anatomy that revealed his age. His face was lined but still handsome, with fine, hawk-like features and eyes that didn't miss a trick. As she took his outstretched hand, his papery old man's skin made her think of a sun-baked lizard.

There was a discreet knock at the door and the waiter entered bearing a tray with silver coffee pot and milk jug and two porcelain cups, which he placed on the low table.

'Good to meet you at last, Elinor! Please sit down. We have coffee here, but if you want something different please say.'

His courtly manner was, she knew, designed to put her at her ease but there was a glint of mischief in his eye that warned her to be on her guard.

'Coffee's fine, thank you.'

'Perhaps I should ask if you've had breakfast?' he said as the waiter continued to hover.

'Thanks. I'm fine.'

Balthus dismissed him with a brief nod of the head and gestured Eli to a seat in one of the armchairs.

'I must apologise for my inhospitality yesterday. So many demands and at my age it is no longer possible to fulfil them. One of the reasons I rarely come to Paris.'

He sat down opposite her.

'I'm grateful to you for fitting me in. I know you must be very busy.'

'Would you mind pouring, Elinor? My hands are a little shaky today.'

Her name sounded oddly intimate on his lips, and his gaze scanned her as she passed him the cup. But when he smiled, his face turned suddenly youthful.

'If I am not mistaken we have met before. Names I forget, but never faces.'

Her heart sank. This was just what she'd hoped to avoid.

'Yes. A couple of years ago. Here in Paris, at the Poussin exhibition.'

'Ah ha!' he declared, triumphant. 'The young woman who claimed to know more about me than I know myself!'

'Hardly. Though I admit it wasn't a good idea, or very polite, to waylay you like that.'

There was a pause as he settled back into his chair and, to her considerable relief, changed the subject.

'I'm sure you have many questions you wish to ask me. But before you do so, I have a confession to make.'

'A confession?'

'I have an aversion to psychoanalysis. In my opinion it is a pseudo science that befuddles more than it clarifies. It claims to provide a motive for everything and in reality says nothing that isn't trite or deluding. People ask me, "What are the sources of your inspiration?"'

She blushed. It was one of the questions she'd been planning to ask.

'I reply they are mysterious and will always remain so. The only thing that matters is the work itself.'

She pulled a notebook and pen from her bag, whilst hunting round in her mind for some other question that might kick off a discussion.

'I understand you never went to art school.'

'No. The Great War made that impossible for many of my generation. But Europe, for all its suffering, still had its museums, churches and galleries with their magnificent art works. What better education for a budding artist?'

'And it was Rilke, I believe, who suggested you study as many of them as possible and make copies. In particular he recommended Piero della Francesca.'

'Rilke was my mentor and Piero my ideal of what a painter can achieve. How a moment of passionate stillness can be made to vibrate forever, poised in that balance between movement and stasis that is eternity. To achieve that is true genius.'

She scribbled a few words as he went on.

'Rilke knew as much about painting as he did about literature. He was the most enlightened human being I ever met, and my friendship with him has been the most significant influence on my life.'

The conversation seemed to be going well, but she reminded herself to tread carefully.

'How old were you when you first met Rilke?'

'Ten or eleven, I don't remember exactly. He was a family friend and took it upon himself to educate me and my brother, something sorely needed in the face of the terrible education system of the time. I hated every minute of school. It taught me nothing and without Rilke it would have been impossible to survive on the starvation rations we received at the hands of our so-called professors.'

He was speaking with unexpected frankness and she began to relax.

'Did you and Rilke spend much time together, or was it mainly a friendship conducted through letters?'

'We met whenever we could. His work was the most important thing to him and for it he required long periods of solitude. But to maintain the friendships that were so important to him, he was a prolific correspondent. He once told me that writing letters was for him like working out for an athlete. It prepared him for the marathon he was about to run when it came to composing poetry.'

'I'm afraid I know relatively little of his poetry, though I'm familiar with his letters.'

'Then you will know that he was as fine a critic as he was a poet, and much valued by Rodin and many other important painters. When I was a boy whenever he came to our apartment, I would show him what I had been working on and he would give detailed comments and encouragement, inspiring me to do better. He had that rare ability of making even someone so much younger than himself feel an equal. Until his death we maintained our dialogue about life and art, face to face and through letters.'

He paused for a moment and his expression softened.

'When he was dying, I was one of the few people he allowed to visit him. Though weak and obviously in pain, we would talk about what we were both working on and his curiosity never failed him.' He paused. 'Sometimes I think it was his generosity of spirit that killed him as much as the disease that racked his body. People used him mercilessly. They drained the life from him!'

She wondered if he was thinking of his mother, Merline, whom Rilke's female friends had been only too ready to accuse of being a succubus. She wanted to bring her into the conversation, but that risked upsetting the mood.

After a pause, she spoke again. 'Rilke's poems often explore the impossible demands of love and friendship. It seems to me that from a different perspective, you deal with a similar theme in your paintings. Men and women inhabiting their own separate spheres.'

His face lost its animation, betraying for a moment his great age, and he replied sharply, 'I do not analyse my work for themes, as you call them.'

'What I mean is, your paintings aren't like that one over there,' she said, gesturing hurriedly towards the Dutch still life. 'Timeless. Dead. Yours live in the moment. They are filled with real feelings, and you make us part of the drama.'

He shrugged. 'I can't explain it to you.'

'You see, even when I know the story behind the images as in your illustrations to *Wuthering Heights*, still there's something more which gives us an added insight into the novel. Some unexplained electricity that's urgent and intensely personal. Why, for example, did you paint yourself as Heathcliff?'

'If I once knew the answer, I no longer remember.'

She pressed on. 'Cathy's self-absorption seems to be provoking Heathcliff to a state of barely suppressed violence, as if he's lost all hope of reaching her. It is a theme you return to again and again.'

She was thinking of all the hours he must have endured as a boy in the claustrophobia of some small flat, doing his best to keep busy by reading or drawing whilst his mother, lost in dreams of her lover, remained oblivious to his existence.

He shifted, growing visibly restless.

'You seem to forget, Elinor. I'm an old man. Such observations confuse me because they have no meaning. Whatever I may have felt at the time is long forgotten. What we have is the painting.'

'But doesn't the controversy some of them still give rise to trouble you? 'The Guitar Lesson', for example? Two women in such an erotically provocative image?'

'You think a young girl's dreams cannot be violent or provocative? Painting is full of violence and eroticism. Caravaggio, for example, a painter I greatly admire, or Rubens, Goya, or Delacroix. I could name many more. The fact that their subject matter is usually religious or classical makes it appear more distant and therefore more acceptable. In the twentieth century our scope has shrunk. Nowadays most dramas take place in a domestic context, and that makes them more intimate and shocking.'

'So such a startling picture is just some girl's imagination? What about your imagination? Doesn't the image of those dreamy girls, oblivious to the world around them, appear only too familiar?'

She waited, expecting an angry rebuttal. Instead he gave a short laugh, followed by a sigh.

'My dear young woman, how intense you are! In its way that is admirable, of course. But it's also exhausting. Unfortunately your questions have no meaning for me, though I see my lack of response causes you frustration and distress. Perhaps that is what we should be talking about?'

He'd turned the tables, pinned her to the wall like a butterfly.

'You're evading the question!'

'Shall I tell you what I see when I look at you? A young woman desperately seeking an answer to what troubles her. For some reason she imagines she may find it in my paintings. But I regret, I cannot help you. Is it not your great William Shakespeare who said, "It is in ourselves that we are thus or thus."?'

'You mean all the suppressed violence I see in your work, the self-absorption that denies the existence of the other, all that is just a reflection of my own feelings? Next you'll tell me that whether we're poor and miserable or a great success is just a manifestation of our own self-image!'

'Yes, in a way. But we were talking about painting.'

She was close to tears, and seeing this he softened.

'My dear girl, you want the truth about what was going on in my mind when I painted those pictures. Truthfully, I do not remember. And what does it matter. If they speak to people with their own voice they will survive. If not they will be forgotten. Do we know what those who built Chartres Cathedral were thinking as they worked, or even who they were? Or what Piero della Francesca had for dinner? Who cares about the artist when they have the work! My work is what I offer you.'

It was true the only thing that mattered was the painting, to be constantly discovered and rediscovered. And if self-belief was what was necessary to achieve anything in this life, then her own lack of it was no doubt what lay behind her failure to fight for what she wanted, and she had no one to blame but herself.

'What is important in your life, Elinor?'

'I'm trying to figure that out. Art matters to me, except I'm not an artist.'

'You are a writer.'

'A journalist. Not a proper writer.'

202

He made an impatient gesture. 'You remind me of my mother. She wanted so much to be a painter but refused to take herself seriously or to make the necessary sacrifice. Her real talent was for life but like many people, she never valued her gifts.'

'I once saw a painting of your mother in Berlin. It was called 'Baladine Dancing'. She was so alive! I've never forgotten it.'

'Yes, in her youth she was a striking woman, though she would not be considered beautiful in these days of the super model. She was too dark, too robust. But she was very graceful and she loved to dance. In a good mood, no one was more joyous.'

His gaze focused on Eli.

'Do not squander your talents.'

'If I manage to discover what they are!'

'I suspect you know very well what they are.'

For a moment she thought he was going to lay his hand on her head in benediction, but it passed and instead he said, 'Perhaps you will come to my exhibition in Rome this summer and we shall talk again.'

'I'll do my best!'

'And now you will return to Berlin? It is not a city I greatly care for, though they tell me it has become quite chic these days amongst the young.'

'I like it a lot.'

'You have a young lover there?'

'Not so young. He's divorced with a son.'

She had a sudden longing for confession.

'Is that a problem?'

'His son has just been sent to prison for being a neo-Nazi.'

'And you are a Jew…'

'Not according to Jewish law. My mother's English.'

He fixed her with his bird-like gaze. 'Sometimes Jews enjoy too much to be victims.'

'That's an outrageous thing to say!'

He shrugged.

'Is the fact that you despise Jews the reason you deny your own Jewish heritage?'

'Now you are angry. I did not mean to provoke you. Any more, by the way, than I despise Jews. You wish to know what is important in life. The only important truths are the creations of the imagination. In life as in art.'

And in accordance with that philosophy, she thought, you invented a title and a palace worthy of yourself at the Villa Medici in Rome. There, you and your fellow fabulist, the film director Federico Fellini, played out your fantasies – the teenage hustler from Rimini and the grandson of a Jewish cantor from Pinsk, neither with the least respect for factual veracity!

Out loud she said, 'You waved your magic wand and invented an outer life to suit the richness of your imagination!'

He grinned like a cat. 'Perhaps I did!'

He got up, a little stiffly. 'I have a favour to ask you before you leave. As a young person more in touch with the times than myself, I would like your opinion on my costume. My wife is giving a fancy dress ball to celebrate the twenty-second birthdays of my daughter and myself. Choosing it was the main reason for my visit to Paris.'

'Twenty-two?'

She was lost.

'Yes. I was born on leap day, so by a strange coincidence my daughter and I find ourselves at exactly the same age.'

He chuckled as he turned away and disappeared into the adjoining room. With his slim, elegant figure standing straight and tall he seemed to have shed fifty years. Perhaps the fact that only twenty-two of his birthdays counted had something to do with his chameleon-like qualities.

A few moments later he emerged clad in an antique red silk kimono, his face hidden by a golden Venetian carnival mask. Its grotesque features with a pronounced beak of a nose seemed to caricature his actual features, giving an impression both louche and menacing. He stood before her like some medieval wizard before removing the mask.

'What do you think?'

'It suits you, though I'm not sure it flatters you.'

'You mean I look grotesque?'

'Let's say, you'll frighten the young girls.'

'Excellent!' he declared, with a mischievous smile.

She smiled too as though suddenly they were fellow conspirators.

'May I ask you a favour in exchange?'

The glance he surveyed her with was faintly mocking. 'Please!'

'D'you mind telling me where your mother is buried?'

He gave a short laugh. 'Is that all? I thought you were about to plumb my deepest secrets!'

'I'm afraid I don't have the skill for that… I'd like to know if there's a grave somewhere.'

He hesitated a second before replying. 'It's in the Bagneux Cemetery, outside the city walls. Not one of the most famous, though the poet Laforgue is buried there and, I believe, Oscar Wilde, until they promoted him to Père Lachaise. I don't advise a visit, though. The place is enormous and you'd need a map to find the tombstone. '

She stood up and stretched out her hand. Leaning towards her as if from a great height, he took it and held it for a moment between long, delicate fingers.

'It's been a great pleasure talking to you – the realisation of a dream!'

He gave a smile in which there was no hint of malice.

'It was a pleasure for me too, Elinor. And don't forget Rome!'

On the way back to the hotel she was buoyed up by an elation both calm and joyous. Balthus had proved every bit as fascinating as she'd imagined, and revealed a capacity for kindness as well as cruelty. She would write something personal that did not descend to the psychologising he so despised but gave the reader an insight into his mercurial intelligence. And she would challenge his more dismissive critics by upholding the serious originality of his art.

There was a message to call Gunter from the hotel receptionist. She glanced at the return ticket lying next to her passport on the bedside table next to the phone, then picked up the receiver and dialled his number. He answered at once.

'Hi! How did the interview go?'

'Good. I'll tell you more when I see you.'

'I wanted to catch you before you left Paris.'

'Why, has something happened?'

'We've got the green light for the film… We're leaving in the morning. I'd hoped to welcome you back, spend a little time together. But now that's impossible. I'm so sorry.'

'Still, it's good news, isn't it?'

He heard the disappointment in her voice. 'Yes. But it wasn't how I'd planned it.'

'How long will you be away?'

'A month. I'll be in touch as soon as I can. We should be back by Easter. I hope you'll still be here. By the way, how did it go with the old man?'

'Good. I'll use the time to get some work done. '

'When I get back we'll go somewhere together. Think about where you'd like it to be.'

There was a brief silence.

'I'll miss you, Eli.'

'You'll be far too busy.'

'That doesn't make me forget you, you funny creature! A month's not long.'

'True… Goodbye then! And good luck with the film!'

'I'll be in touch as soon as I can. Keep the bed warm for me!'

She replaced the receiver and leaned back against the pillow, fighting tears. The news that Gunter would be gone when she returned caught her unawares, erasing her elation. At the same time she asked herself what stupidity had prevented her from telling him how much she loved and would miss him. Was she so insecure she was afraid he might not return, or if he did it would be to tell her his feelings had changed? She thought of Merline and Rilke's passionate outpourings in letter after letter, without reserve or inhibition. It was quite possible such heightened language, with its exaggerated forms of expression and elaborate poetic conceits, wasn't really a true reflection of their feelings but owed more to the imagination.

She got up, reached for her suitcase and began to pack.

Châtillon-Montrouge was the end of the metro line and Bagneux Cemetery only a short walk away. Visiting Merline's grave was an act of homage she wanted to make before leaving Paris. There might even be some echo of her presence in this, her final resting place. The day was crisp and bright but once out of the city it felt several degrees colder with an underlying chill that threatened to get into the bones. She pulled up the collar of her coat. The pamphlet she'd picked up at the station said the cemetery was sometimes known as the Jewish Cemetery because of the large number of Jews buried there, and there were also memorials to Jews killed in the Second World War and the Warsaw Ghetto. She wondered if it had been Pierre's decision to bury his mother there.

She entered the gates and walked down a bleak, tree-lined avenue that seemed to stretch to infinity, with graves on either side as far as the eye could see. After walking for what seemed like miles she sat down on a stone bench, covered with needles from the great cedar that overspread it. Her gaze wandered over the sea of tombstones, some lovingly tended with vases of fresh or plastic flowers, others their inscriptions worn away or obscured by moss. She appeared to be the only visitor and, given the size of the place, finding Merline's grave would be like looking for a needle in a haystack.

Searching round, she spotted a gardener's hut and set off in its direction. Inside she found a man in uniform brewing up tea. He welcomed her in and began proudly reeling off a list of famous people who lay there under his charge. Cutting him short, she asked if he could direct her to the tomb of Baladine Klossowska. At first he claimed not to know of her but eventually he produced a dog-eared map of the cemetery, containing a list of all its inhabitants. Merline was in the ninety-eighth section.

She walked down alleys, past simple graves and ornate tombs, some gated and topped with grieving statues, others pillared with cherubs holding aloft marble scrolls. At last she came to one of the most neglected aisles at the far end of the cemetery and stopped before a plain, weather-beaten headstone, on which was engraved the name Baladine Klossowska in simple characters. She brushed aside the dried leaves piled against it and knelt down, running her fingers over the indentations in the lichen-covered stone. The stone wasn't cold like marble but had a breathing quality, almost like a living organism. She waited, willing some sense of Merline's presence to manifest itself, but none came. She thought of her finding refuge after so turbulent a life in this quiet place amongst others of her suffering tribe, and prayed she had at last found peace.

She was roused from her reverie by the sound of a bell announcing the closing of the cemetery. It took a while to reach the gate where the guard was waiting, impatient to lock up. She bid him good night and set off once again for the metro. At a bend in the road a flock of rooks took flight noisily from the bare branches of a clump of trees. She watched them as they swept upwards, black against the yellow remains of a winter sunset into the darkening sky, where a crescent moon was emerging from behind ragged clouds.

Berlin, 1996
In The Dungeon Of Love

Entering the flat, she was overwhelmed by its emptiness. The open books that littered every surface in the living room and the lingering smell of Gunter's dark tobacco shouted out his absence. She realised that after two years of spending more and more of her time here, she'd made no impression on the place. Books, furniture, pictures, CDs and DVDs were all his. Only the table in the bedroom she'd commandeered as a work desk and a few clothes in the hanging cupboard were testimony to her ever having been there.

She'd told herself that, like the cat that comes and goes, she preferred things that way. Now, as she wandered disconsolately through the empty rooms on which she'd made so little impression, she understood the price of her detachment and longed for some sign that 'his' had become 'ours'. In the bedroom a pile of dirty clothes lay abandoned in a corner but fresh sheets had been laid out on the bed. She picked up the clothes, burying her face to breathe in the familiar odour of his body, and was seized by a yearning so powerful she had to sit down on the bed and wait for it to pass. For over a year he'd been obsessed with the labyrinthine problems of raising finance for his film. Now he had it, might he not disappear for two months, three, even six? And all she could do was wait.

She went into the kitchen. Jars of spices from something he'd cooked were lined up next to the cooker. The crockery had been washed and left to dry on the draining board, though he'd neglected to empty the bins. A jar of blue anemones stood on the table. She recognised it as a gesture of welcome, but there was no note with its guarantee of words. She flicked through the pile of letters on the table. The two for herself she put on one side. She'd check the rest later for bills or anything important. She was here to write and must stick to her resolve. Meanwhile she needed to find a part-time job if she was to have enough to live on.

She listened to the answerphone messages in case he'd called. There was a hasty one from Nairobi airport as he waited for a connecting flight, saying he'd try again as soon as they reached Blantyre. She wasn't particularly hungry but made scrambled eggs then put her plate in the sink, cleaned her teeth and went to bed. In the morning she woke with a headache, having forgotten to open the window and the heating as usual was turned up too high for someone brought up in a land of draughts. She made coffee, which she drank at the kitchen table and flicked through the ads in the paper she'd picked up at the airport, but found nothing of interest. The best way to find work was to go round the local bars and cafés in person.

She put on a heavy coat, gloves and fur cap against the bitter cold, and left the house. Clouds had clamped down over the city like a lid and people scurried by, doing their best to get back indoors as soon as possible. When it snowed, the streets came alive. Blue shadows turned apricot and pink in the low sun that reflected off the windows of surrounding buildings. But now the snow had shrunk to mounds of blackened slush, piled up at the edges of gritty pavements.

As she passed the Turkish market that ran alongside the canal, strings of lights and the chatter of stallholders gave a welcome cheer to the gloomy day. One of the traders, a thickset middle-aged man wearing a sheepskin cap with earflaps and fingerless gloves, gave her his usual friendly greeting. She often stopped at his stall to buy one of his sweet, silty coffees, heated three times on an open flame in a small copper pot, and a delicious honey pastry. Sometimes they fell into conversation and she knew he ran one of the cafés further down the street, with the help of his wife and son.

'Haven't seen you for a while, missy,' he said, handing her a coffee in a thick white china cup. 'You keep well, I hope?'

'Yes. I've been in Paris.'

'Ah, Paris! City of joy! And now you are back.'

'And looking for work. D'you know of anything part time?'

He paused for a moment then said, 'My wife is in hospital for a small operation. It is likely we need someone for help in the café. If you like I speak to my son. He runs things there.'

'That would be great. Shall I come back tomorrow?'

'Yes. This time tomorrow.'

She finished her coffee and moved on to buy what she needed from the fruit and vegetable stall. Most of the café's customers during the day were young people and parents out shopping with their children. In the evenings and on Sundays the Turkish men took over, with their hubble-bubbles and card games, but she doubted she'd be required to work then. If the hours were right the job would be perfect.

When she got home, she put away her shopping and set about preparing soup for the maultaschen she'd developed a taste for. While the soup cooked, she transferred her work papers from the bedroom to the kitchen table, and thought what a relief it would be to spend a few hours each day in some lively, friendly place. Outside, a crescent moon and a sprinkling of cold stars were visible through the bare branches of the sycamore tree, where grey-headed crows crouched like harpies.

She picked up her mother's letter and was skimming through trivial items of family news when the phone rang. She snatched it up, thinking it would be Gunter. With a shock she recognised Malgorzata's voice.

'Eli? Hi. I rang earlier but no one was in. Has Gunter left for Africa yet?'

'Oh, hi! Yes, a couple of days ago.'

'Damn! How long will he be away?'

'Till Easter.'

'A month!'

'Maybe longer. Is there a problem?'

'Well, yes. Bruno's been granted early parole from the Young Offenders' Institute for good behaviour. They're keen to get rid of some of the less serious cases.'

'That's good news!'

'Yes, except that I'm booked to go to Greece on Monday, and as usual Gunter isn't around. I've been commissioned to do a mosaic for an environmental centre in Corinth.'

'So what are you saying?'

There was a pause before Malgorzata continued.

'I was wondering if Bruno might come and stay with you, until Gunter gets back?'

Eli was silent.

'Hallo? Are you there?'

'Sorry! Stay with me, did you say? What about the authorities?'

'They wouldn't need to be involved. He's just turned eighteen and he's under the care of his probation officer. It would simply be a matter of a change of address. That is if it's OK with you.'

'Have you asked Bruno?'

'He says it's fine. He doesn't want to live with me any more and would prefer to go to his father. Besides he likes you.'

Eli's head was spinning.

'How can he like me? I've only met him once... And he hates Jews!'

'That makes it all the more important.'

She was about to retort that she didn't see herself as part of Bruno's rehabilitation programme and anyway she was far too busy, when Malgorzata spoke again.

'Sorry. That came out wrong. What I mean is, he doesn't

really know what he thinks because he has no experience. At heart, despite all the crap he's been filling himself with, he's a good, gentle boy. If I didn't believe that, I wouldn't suggest this for a minute.'

'But what would I do with him?'

'You wouldn't have to do anything. He's at work all day and at night he has to observe a nine o'clock curfew. He knows what's at stake if he breaks the rules, and being back inside isn't an experience he's keen to repeat. Truly, I wouldn't ask if I thought he'd be a problem. And it'll be a chance for him to make things up with Gunter!'

That bit, at least, was true. Gunter would jump at the chance of a reconciliation that otherwise might never take place. She needed time to think.

'This is a bit sudden. Let me call you back in the morning.'

The rest of the evening passed in turmoil. Just when she'd made plans to earn the money she needed with sufficient time for writing, she was being asked to take on a boy she had no interest in or affection for. The presence of anyone in the flat, let alone Bruno, would be disruptive. At the same time if she was serious about her commitment to Gunter, how could she deny him the chance he longed for to repair the damage he believed he'd inflicted on his son? Sharing a life with Gunter meant accepting his child and in the general scheme of things a month wasn't long, though in these circumstances it felt like eternity. She tried calling him but his mobile had no connection and the production office in Berlin had an answerphone message saying it was temporarily closed. She decided to sleep on it.

After a restless night she woke with a start, conscious that Malgorzata was waiting for an answer and she herself was due at ten at the Turkish café. She picked up the phone and after a couple of rings Malgorzata answered.

'I'll accept Bruno providing I've got personal authorisation from his probation officer. I also need it to be understood that if he infringes the least condition of his parole, I'll report him and he'll be straight back in prison. I hope that's clear?'

'Thanks, Eli! I can't tell you how pleased he'll be, and how grateful I am.'

There was no going back now, and the relief in Malgorzata's voice was palpable. She had, she told herself, done the right thing.

They agreed for the handover to take place on Sunday when Bruno wouldn't be at the supermarket where he was now employed. They met at a pizza joint in Kurfurstendamm. Malgorzata was lively and talkative but Bruno said almost nothing, despite Eli's efforts to draw him into the conversation. When they had finished eating and emerged onto the street, he said goodbye to his mother with little sign of emotion. His silence as he and Eli walked off in the direction of the U-Bahn gave her a feeling of near panic about what she'd taken on.

'D'you want to go somewhere for a coffee or shall we go straight home?'

'Might as well go to the apartment. It's freezing and I'd like to dump my rucksack.'

She noted how he avoided the word 'home'. His cheeks were blotchy and shoulders hunched with cold. His leather jacket was clearly inadequate for the sudden drop in temperature.

During the ride on the U-Bahn Eli asked him about his job. He answered politely but offered nothing, so she soon gave up. If this went on, how would they get through the rest of the day, let alone four weeks?

She'd stocked the fridge with things she thought a lad his age would like, and put clean sheets and a handmade quilt on the bed in the guest room in an effort to make the place welcoming. As soon as she spoke to Gunter she'd get him to make a firm commitment about his return date. Until then they would have to make the best of it. After an early supper Bruno said he was going to his room; he had to be up early for work in the morning. She heard him shifting around, then silence. Assuming he'd fallen asleep, she decided to turn in herself. A poor night and the stress of the day made nothing so desirable as falling unconscious.

The following morning she got up earlier than usual, intending to make breakfast. It was important to establish some sort of routine. But Bruno had already left for work. It was her first day at the Turkish café so after coffee and toast, she distracted herself until it was time to leave by tidying up the flat. She'd agreed to work there weekdays from ten till three, which left time to do her own stuff after her shift.

She arrived at the café five minutes early. It was already half full of women with toddlers and a few men reading newspapers or working on their laptops. Yusuf, the stallholder, was there to greet her. His son, he said, didn't arrive till six but he introduced her to his elderly mother, an old woman in shapeless black relieved only by an incongruously garish headscarf. She nodded curtly but didn't smile or speak. Yusuf explained that she didn't speak German but looked after the books and knew the business inside out. She sat next to the cash till at the end of the counter as if guarding it, a magazine at her elbow covered in grids and squares and Turkish letters.

'Puzzles!' Yusuf said, gesturing towards it. 'She does them to keep her mind sharp. Not that she needs it!'

He took Eli into the kitchen and introduced her to Kamal, who did the cooking and took care of the dishwasher. Kamal spoke a little German and, unlike the old woman, was friendly and welcoming. Her duties would be to clear the tables and serve the customers. If there were communication problems Yusuf's nine-year-old granddaughter, Fatimah, returned from school just after twelve each day and spoke the language fluently. In case of an emergency he, Yusuf, could be found at his stall. With that he handed her a snowy white apron, wished her luck and hurried off.

For the rest of the morning she was kept busy with a steady flow of customers. She hadn't worked serving food since a summer job at Butlin's Holiday Camp at the end of her first year at university. All she recalled of that was sore feet and the rancid smell of cooking fat that permanently pervaded her clothes and hair and even the tacky hut she slept in. Here at least the smells were spicy and more appetising.

At midday the steady flow turned into a rush and, as the orders piled up and people waited impatiently at uncleared tables, she was intensely grateful to see young Fatimah. Her competence, it turned out, far exceeded her own. When scurrying back and forth to the kitchen, she dropped a plate from the pile she was carrying. Before she had time to dump the rest and fetch a cloth Fatimah had the mess cleared up. Another time she almost lost her cool with a mother who changed her child's order three times. When finally she set down a plate of egg and chips in front of him, the child set up a deafening wail of complaint and the mother berated her for not listening to the customer. Fatimah appeared from nowhere with a plate of pasta and meatballs. She placed it in front of the boy, who rewarded her with a smile.

'Don't worry. That kid's a brat!' she said, as they retreated to the kitchen. 'As long as Grandma's not looking, we'll eat the egg and chips ourselves. Grandma's a witch!'

By three o'clock Eli was exhausted, and decided to go straight home for a hot shower before making dinner for herself and Bruno.

He returned at around six, ate the supper she put in front of him as though half starved, washed up his plate and retired to his room. She had put Gunter's old computer in there and he had his Walkman for listening to music. She paused outside his door to listen but there was no sound. He was probably asleep. If he continued to spend so much time in there it would make life easier, but that wasn't what she'd committed to when she'd taken him on.

The second day at the café was easier as she familiarised herself with the routine. Around twelve there was a brief lull as the breakfasters gave way to the lunchtime crowd, and she had time for one of Kamal's coffees and a sandwich and chat with Fatimah. She was amazed how mature and self-possessed the child was and found herself talking to her like an adult. She even mentioned having Bruno, her boyfriend's son and a complete stranger, staying with her at the apartment. Fatimah asked if she liked him and she answered truthfully, not much so far, though she hoped things would improve.

When she'd finished her stint at the café she decided to go to the museum library for a couple of hours and reread the letters Merline had written to Rilke on her return to Paris. Their description of those precious last weeks together, which had had to suffice Merline for the rest of her long life, never failed to move her.

'*My dearest friend,*' she wrote in her final letter to him:

Those quiet days together meant so much to me, René, so much that I cannot put into words. I must believe that you have found the strength you need to finish your great work. The world waits, holding its breath, for the rich gift you have in store for it. I picture you in your room so filled with light, writing at your lectern or walking in the garden at the end of the day amongst the last of the roses. Think of me, darling, oh, think of me, as their scent tenderly envelops you, and believe the profound gratitude I feel for every fleeting moment of the inexpressible joy we shared.

In her earlier encounters with these letters she'd had the uncomfortable sensation of being a voyeur in another's intimate life. But reading and rereading them, her feeling for Merline had developed into something closer, as though they'd become friends. If she could, she would have asked her what to do about Bruno, sure of wise counsel hard won from her experience with her own unruly son.

When she got home Bruno was already there.

'Supper won't be long. I hope you're hungry,' she remarked cheerily.

'It's OK. You don't have to wait on me. My mother left food in the fridge. I'm quite capable of making my own meals.'

'Eating together is an important part of living together,' she retorted. 'A time to talk and get to know each other.'

It was essential to establish some ground rules. The mere ten years that separated them made her determined to emphasise they were neither friends nor flatmates.

'This is supposed to be a shared home, not a hostel. If I'm cooking for myself, I might as well do so for you. Let's say I cook and you wash up.'

He said nothing, so she spelt out a list of chores.

'You carry down the rubbish, put your dirty clothes and bed linen in the washing machine and clean the apartment once a week. How does that sound?'

'If that's what you want.'

Irritated, she turned away.

It was a relief that for the next couple of days they saw little of each other. The only connection they shared was through the man of whom neither spoke, yet whose absence was like a gaping hole in the centre of the room around which they circled as strangers. Physically, Bruno resembled his mother and she could detect little of Gunter, except his profile and occasionally a quizzical expression when she caught him observing her. When she got up in the morning he'd already left for work and at night, after a hasty meal eaten in virtual silence, he went to bed. If she asked about his day he responded in monosyllables. He had dark rings under his eyes and by the end of the meal seemed scarcely able to keep them open. He showed no curiosity about what she did all day and most likely wasn't aware she worked at the Turkish café.

One evening at supper he looked her straight in the eye and said, 'I've been meaning to ask. Does Gunter know I'm staying here with you?'

She noted his avoidance of the word 'father'.

'I haven't managed to reach him yet. But he's often said how much it would mean to him if you were to come and stay.'

'Still he's not here, is he?'

'He will be soon… And I'm happy to do what he wants.'

'Lucky him!' He paused. 'Are you two planning to get married?'

'It's not something we've thought about so far.'

His tone infuriated her. 'Is that all the questions for now?'

'Yes, I think so,' he replied coolly.

Towards Bruno she felt alternating indifference and hostility. His alien presence filled the flat, destroying her peace of mind and with it her concentration. By contrast, the noise and camaraderie of the café was a blessed relief, and in particular Fatimah. When she returned after work she was invariably greeted by the sound of mindless chatter from some TV programme, and found him in the living room slumped in front of it. He made an excuse and disappeared to his own room, leaving her rummaging for the controls in an effort to extinguish the screen. To offer more meaningful diversion she suggested that at the weekend he and she might go to a museum together or see a film.

'It must be boring for you, stuck here all the time by yourself.'

'I'm fine,' he replied. 'Please don't trouble yourself about me.'

He was like a fish constantly slipping from her grasp. The only moment of open dissension was when she suggested he look for more interesting work than filling shelves at a supermarket.

'Obviously you don't understand the employment situation in Germany. Jobs the unions haven't got sewn up, the government hand out to foreigners. There's nothing for the rest of us Germans.'

'You don't really believe "foreigners" are the cause of Germany's economic ills?' she retorted, unable to keep the sarcasm out of her voice. 'There's work out there, if you bothered to look. Or you could go to university or get an apprenticeship.'

But he'd already closed off.

No one phoned him or dropped round, even though he'd lived in the city all his life. As far as she knew only his mother had contacted him since his arrival, calling up to see how he was once she'd arrived in Greece. Eli marvelled at the ruthlessness with which she'd grabbed her freedom, offloading her son into the care of strangers without a backward glance. If it was an attempt to get back at Gunter it had misfired, leaving her the target, and for the umpteenth time she asked herself how she could possibly have agreed to the arrangement.

A couple of days later at the café she came across a music magazine someone had left behind and, flicking through it, saw a photo of Bruno's band in an article describing the current punk scene. The writer referred to their music as the energetic voice of Germany's disaffected youth, though he also made reference to rumoured associations with the far right. Despite that, it was clear he took their music seriously. She decided to take it home as a peace offering.

Bruno seized on it, becoming almost vociferous. The band, he said, was planning to bring out a single, which if it did well might lead to an album.

'D'you miss playing?'

'It's the only thing that means anything to me!' he retorted, and for the first time she felt a flicker of sympathy. It wasn't fun living under curfew with his father's mistress and filling shelves in a supermarket, when the only thing he cared about had been taken away.

'No doubt you'd say I brought it on myself.'

'Well, didn't you?'

He got up, turned on his heel and left the room. For the first time he'd dropped his mask of polite cool. Perhaps now, she thought, they might start talking to one another.

Yet the following evening nothing had changed. They ate their supper in silence, except for the odd remark such as, 'How was your day?' to which he answered, 'Fine,' or 'Pass the salt,' which required no verbal response. As a result for the next few days she went to the gym after work to tire herself out on the machines and put off the moment of return. She took her supper into the living room and ate it in front of the TV news then retired to the bathroom, where she ran a bath and stayed there in the cooling water until she heard his bedroom door shut. The flat felt like a bubble cut off from the rest of the world, in which the two of them were cocooned. She'd scarcely written a word since his arrival, except a draft synopsis for her article, and she was counting the days until Easter.

It occurred to her that Bruno might be clinically depressed and she asked Fatimah at the café what she did when she wanted to cheer herself up.

'You're sad?' the girl asked, concerned.

'Not me. Bruno. It's hardly surprising. What would you do if your parents went away and left you with Grandma.'

'I'd not stay with her. She only likes boys.'

'But would it cheer you up to go swimming in the lake, or to the cinema, or with your friends to that new ice cream parlour in Mitte?'

She considered a moment. 'The circus! Not the ones with lions and tigers, but acrobats on high wires. What do you call them?'

'Trapeze artists?'

'Yes!' She clapped her hands in delight. 'That's what I'd be if I could be anything I wanted. A trapeze artist!'

It wasn't much help. There was no circus in town, and she doubted Bruno would share Fatimah's enthusiasm for acrobats.

On Saturday when he was at work, Eli was putting laundry into the washing machine and noticed semen stains on his sheet. She was seized by a wave of revulsion. Hitherto he'd appeared to her as a sort of androgynous Peter Pan, barely on the verge of manhood. It hadn't occurred to her he might have sexual desires and she found herself behaving towards him even more irritably than ever. When at length she caught sight of her sour face in the hall mirror she felt ashamed.

What would Gunter think if he could see her now? She'd finally managed to get through to him and he'd declared his undying gratitude for her generosity in looking after his son. He suggested all three of them might take a trip to the Alps at Easter and at once all tender feelings evaporated. She asked herself furiously what kind of cloud cuckoo land he was living in, imagining them going off together to play Happy Families in the Alps.

A couple of evenings later she came home and found Bruno seated at the kitchen table, gouging out an intricate pattern in preparation for a linocut. She stood watching him from the doorway, biting his lip with concentration, the fine lines of his cheekbones highlighted by the lamp, and the Roman arch of his nose reminiscent of his father's. The lashes of his lowered eyelids were long and thick like a girl's and for a moment he reminded her of a fawn from some classical painting, half man, half satyr. She stood still, not wanting to break the spell of his concentration, until he looked up and gave one of his rare smiles with no hint of mockery.

'I came across this stuff in a cupboard at the supermarket. It would have been thrown away, so I cut it up and brought it home.'

'Where did you learn to do linocutting?'

'Malgorzata taught me when I was a kid… The only good stuff that shithole's got to offer!'

She watched him ink and roll the prepared lino and thought, not for the first time, how little she understood him. He handed her the print he'd made to inspect. It was remarkable how delicately he'd managed to depict the boughs of the tree and dull sheen of a crow's plumage.

'You've got real talent!' She returned the paper. 'Have you ever thought of going to art school?'

'My mother says I should. I suppose it'd be better than the supermarket. But for now that's what I'm stuck with.'

It was the first time he'd said anything about art school. She wasn't sure if he was serious or whether it was just something else to soften her up.

The work seemed to liberate his tongue and he began telling her about things that had happened during the day, mimicking the pompous speech of the store manager trying to calm an irate customer, and very soon she was laughing. They were interrupted by the sound of the doorbell.

She went to the intercom. It was Fatimah. She pressed the buzzer and opened the door of the flat. Leaning over the banister she watched the small figure trudging up the stairs and called out a welcome.

'Hey! This is a surprise!'

Fatimah, panting, reached the top and held out an envelope.

'It's Friday. You forgot your wages. You'd better check it's all there.'

'That's kind of you, but it could have waited till Monday.'

'Dad said you might need the money for the weekend… Aren't you going to count it?'

'I'm sure it's all there. D'you want to come in for a minute?'

The child peered past her into the flat. 'OK. Just for a minute.'

She stood aside and Fatimah entered.

Bruno looked up at the small, dark girl who followed Eli into the kitchen.

'This is Fatimah. Fatimah, Bruno. Can I get you something to drink, some cordial perhaps?'

'Yes, please.'

She went over to the table where Bruno was working on his next linocut, and stood watching in silent fascination. Eli glanced at the two of them as she mixed the cordial and the world suddenly seemed normal.

'How d'you make those lines?' Fatimah asked.

'You cut the lino with this tool, then ink it with the roller and press some paper on top of the ink to make a print.'

'Can you show me?'

Bruno inked the piece of lino he'd been working on and placed a piece of paper onto it. He handed the dry roller to Fatimah.

'Now press down with that. Be careful not to move the paper or it'll smudge.'

With great care Fatimah did as she was told, a fierce look of concentration on her face. When she'd finished she stood back and Bruno carefully lifted the paper off the lino. She stared at the image of crows on a bare branch in amazement.

'Wow! I'd like to learn to do that.'

She looked at him admiringly.

'You can have some of these lino squares and a bottle of ink. You'll have to find paper and a roller for yourself. A potato peeler works quite well to gouge out the lino.'

She nodded. 'My dad'll find them for me, if I ask him.'

Eli handed her the cordial, which she swallowed down in a single gulp.

'I'd better go now. I said I wouldn't be long. Thanks for the drink.' She took the lino and ink bottle from Bruno. 'And for these.'

'You're welcome.'

'Hang on. I'll get you a bag,' Eli said.

Rootling round in the cupboard under the sink, she brought out one of Bruno's supermarket carriers.

She accompanied Fatimah to the front door and watched her as she descended the stairs. When she returned to the kitchen, Bruno was washing ink off pieces of lino and tidying up his tools.

'Bright little thing,' he remarked.

'Isn't she... for a foreigner!'

'Let's hope she escapes the usual fate of Turkish women.'

And for once she didn't disagree.

'You think I'm just some thick racist, don't you?'

'No! Well, I think you have your prejudices.'

'The Turks have gangs too, you know. They rule the streets in this neighbourhood and don't think much of the rest of us. Especially immigrants, Romanians, Somalis, even East Germans.'

'East Germans are hardly immigrants.'

'To the Turks they are. They're commies, freeloaders, out like the rest of them for what they can get.'

'And aren't the Turks? In search of a better life?'

'Maybe. But now they're not the only ones. Too many rats in a cage and they'll fight each other to the death.'

'So they, like you, want Germany for the Germans, plus the Turks!'

'You can joke if you like. You're not out there.'

'Is that why you don't go out?'

'I've got a curfew.'

As usual their conversation got nowhere. She glanced again at his lino cuts laid out on the table waiting for the ink to dry. She wanted to say something that would redeem the moment and prevent it from turning sour, but could think of nothing.

Later, when she was making supper, he entered the kitchen with the volume of Balthus paintings that had been lying on her desk in the sitting room.

'Is this what you spend your days poring over? All these dozy girls with their skirts pulled up over their fannies!'

'D'you like them?' she replied, adopting a friendly tone.

'Not much.'

She stopped what she was doing, went to the table and

opened up the book at an image entitled, 'Thérèse Dreaming'. A young girl sits in a chair, hands joined behind her head, one leg crooked rucking up her skirt, eyes closed. At her feet a white cat licks at a saucer of milk.

'Look! Even though she's half asleep, she's so alive. You can almost feel her breathing.'

He gazed at the picture, his expression unreadable. She turned over the page to reveal another image showing the enclosed end of a street, 'Le Passage du Commerce Saint-André'. A tall man carrying a baguette under one arm is walking away from the viewer. In the background a bent old woman shuffles along a path that will bring her into collision with the man, and in the foreground a small white dog sniffs the ground and some odd-looking children play on the pavement. On the opposite side of the street a bald man sits hugging his knees with his feet in the gutter. None of them looks at the retreating figure with the bread, yet his presence dominates the scene.

'What about this one?' she asked.

'What about it?'

'That man holding the bread. He's anonymous and at the same time holds the rest of them in his power.'

He looked more closely.

'He's the painter,' she continued. 'Or how the painter sees himself, like the ringmaster in a circus.'

He turned his head to look at her. 'How do you know all that?'

'I've looked at these paintings so often.'

'Have you ever met the artist?'

'Briefly. He's very old now.'

'And pretty weird!'

'Not particularly. Does that matter?'

Bruno shrugged.

The fact that he came to the paintings without preconceptions made his responses all the more intriguing. 'The Room' and 'The Guitar Lesson' he dismissed as pornography. Others, where the sexual tension was less explicit, he liked because they challenged conventional romanticism.

'D'you think Balthus hates women or loves them?' he asked, gazing at an illustration for *Wuthering Heights*.

'Good question! Both probably. Like most men.'

'Women always think they're right!'

'You think men don't?'

'My grandfather called them witches.'

'Witches! I wonder why that doesn't surprise me.'

'In his language the word means sorcerer.'

'Oh, I see! Balthus thought of himself as a kind of sorcerer, or shapeshifter. Sometimes he's the watching cat in the corner there, sometimes the dwarf-like woman pulling back the curtains or even the dreamy girl. In this one,' she turned back to the *Wuthering Heights* illustration, 'he paints himself as Heathcliff.'

'All painters are really painting themselves, according to my mother.'

'In Balthus' case his fantasies spilled over into his life and he turned himself into a prince!'

'You mean his paintings made him rich and successful.'

'I mean he created a whole new history for himself, and a set of fictitious noble ancestors. In reality he was just the grandson of a Jewish cantor from Pinsk.'

Bruno was silent. The notion that such a wholesale transformation might be possible appeared to intrigue him.

'It was from the Jewish side he got his talent. Also his great belief in himself. Yet he denied that part of his family, and with it most of his history. And he rejected any old friends who refused to go along with his fiction.'

'I guess if you reject your past, it makes sense to create a whole new history for yourself. He obviously felt it was worth it.'

'It's never worth it!'

'How do you know?'

'You lose all sense of who you are. You can't just decide to be someone else.'

'Why not, if you hate who you are?... So why d'you think Balthus did it?'

'I often ask myself, and I don't know the answer.'

'If we can't change the world, we change ourselves.'

'Maybe. Perhaps it's something dreamers do.' She was going to say 'fantasists', but that sounded too disparaging.

He got up and went over to the window. When he turned back, his eyes seemed veiled in a face that had the untouched pallor of a mask.

'If an artist creates a world out of his imagination, why shouldn't he live in it? What's so important about your so-called reality?'

'What about the people around him? Do they have to live in it too?'

'That's up to them... I'm off to bed.'

'Don't you want to eat something first?'

He shook his head. 'I'm not hungry.'

'OK... Sleep well,' she added.

That night between sleep and wakefulness, strange dreams swam in and out of her consciousness. Great undulating swathes of material, some rough to the touch, some silky smooth, swelled around her as she slithered down into the crevices between soft billows and was almost smothered, only to be bounced aloft and tumble back once more. Bruno was there, though she couldn't see him. She called out to him but her voice made no sound, and it was a relief when she woke.

Their conversation about the paintings seemed to have opened up a channel of communication. The following evening as they sat at supper, he looked up at her and said, 'Do you love my father?'

'Very much. Why?'

'Just curious.'

'He's a good man and there aren't too many of those.'

'Is he?'

'You know he is! If you didn't think so, why did you want to come and live with him?'

He paused for a moment then said, 'I came here to kill him.'

She was so shocked she didn't know whether to laugh or to grab him by the throat. Such random provocation might be his stock in trade but it destroyed at a stroke whatever trust had been building.

'Why would you want to do that?' she said with forced calm.

'How else can I free myself of the past?'

'I should have thought killing your father would have the opposite effect. It would lock you into the past forever.'

Alone in her room she punched the bed pillows in silent fury. Eventually she sat up and took some deep, calming breaths. She had little doubt this was just another of Bruno's stupid, melodramatic gestures, but it made a mockery of her hopes of bringing about a reconciliation between him and Gunter. If she told him it would shatter his belief in the possibility of a rapprochement, yet she could hardly keep it to herself. It was too late to call Malgorzata in Greece, and what would she say? 'Your son says he intends to kill his father!' She might inform the authorities and tell them she was afraid Bruno might be violent and insist they take him back into custody. But that too would destroy any hope of a future, and in any case she didn't really believe it. She lay on the bed, staring into the darkness. Love seemed so easy when there were just two of you.

In the morning, bleary from lack of sleep, she lay in bed until she heard the front door close then forced herself to get up, made coffee and dressed. She wasn't due at the café for another hour and walked the streets, slippery with spring rain. Buds were forming between the forlorn remnants of Christmas lights still threaded through the boughs of trees. A group of schoolchildren were throwing missiles at the swans on the canal. The birds took off with a clumsy beating of wings, treading water in ungainly haste before laboriously taking to the air. The children laughed and searched around for further ammunition. This morning it was all too easy to understand Merline's hatred for the city.

When midday came Fatimah failed to arrive at the café. Nor was she there by three o'clock when it was time for Eli to leave. She'd never missed a day before and she asked Kamal if anything had happened to the girl. He replied in broken German that she had a cold.

When she got home, she poured herself a glass of wine and sat down to wait for Bruno. She gave no thought to food or what to prepare for dinner. Anger had solidified into resolution. She would make him talk whatever it took. Half an hour later she heard his key in the door and he entered the kitchen.

'Hi! What's for supper? I'm starving!' His manner was artlessly innocent.

'Sit down, Bruno. I want to talk to you.'

'Can I make a cup of tea first?'

'Just sit down!'

At the sound of her raised voice, he lifted his hands in a gesture of 'pax' and took a seat opposite her.

'When I agreed to accept you here it was to prevent you from having to return to prison, and you agreed to abide by the terms of your parole. Is it true you've been seeing your probation officer regularly and going to work?'

'Of course! What's all this about?'

He sounded so aggrieved it was all she could do not to grab him and shake the life out of him. Never before had she felt such desire for physical violence.

'What have you told your probation officer about why you wanted to come and live with your father?'

'That's between him and me, isn't it?'

'Answer the fucking question! Otherwise I'll call him right now and tell him I'm not prepared to go on with this farce. You'll be back inside before your feet touch the ground.'

'I've done nothing wrong.'

'Nor will you, if I've got anything to do with it.'

He paused for a moment then said, 'I told him I wanted to see if my dad and I could work out our problems. He agreed it was worth a try.'

'Did you tell him you hated your father?'

'Lots of kids say they hate their parents.'

'They don't all say they're going to kill them.'

'Oh, come on! Isn't that what all the psycho docs say? We need to kill the tyrant within!'

She swallowed hard in an effort to remain calm.

'I'm sick of your games, Bruno, and I'm warning you. If I think you're a danger to your father or anyone else I'm going straight to the police. Is that clear?'

'OK.' His tone was irritatingly meek.

'That isn't just an empty threat! If I don't trust you, I can't have you living here, and I'm not prepared to take the risk.'

'You're seriously worried I'm going to kill my father?' He made it sound ridiculous.

'Why the hell say it if you didn't mean it?'

'I guess I wanted to see how you'd react… D'you want me to leave?'

'Is that all you ever want, a reaction? D'you think that's the only way people can relate to one another?'

He gazed at her with his cool, appraising look. 'When people are provoked, they're less likely to lie. Take you. You tell me you want me here for the sake of my dad. In fact it's the last thing you want – me intruding into your happy little life with Gunter.'

She was shocked into momentary silence.

'It's OK.' He went on in a reassuring tone. 'We can share the apartment till my probation ends, then I'll be out of your hair.'

'Whatever you think of me, it's his place and he wants you here,' she protested.

She'd underestimated his intelligence and felt herself at a disadvantage.

'My parents wanted to show the world how talented they were. They didn't have time for a child,' he said, after a pause.

'They loved you, though.'

He shrugged. 'Most of the time I was invisible.'

She thought of Balthus telling his mother how without Rilke's dedication to his little book about his cat Mitsou, his teacher, M. Pittard, would have doubted his very existence. Her own experience couldn't have been more different, with parents and grandparents who'd left her in no doubt of her importance in their lives.

'I understand Gunter feels guilty, but that doesn't matter any more.'

She tried to think of a reply but none came to her. What he said was true. She got up. 'It's late. I'm going to bed. We'll talk again tomorrow.'

'Goodnight.'

As she left the room she felt his eyes on her back, but resisted the impulse to turn round.

Some hours later she was woken by a strong wind that blew up from the east, bringing a belated blizzard. Something was banging. She tried to ignore it but at length got up to investigate. The fastener to one of the metal shutters in the kitchen had come loose so that it swung to and fro. Through the window in the street below a whirlwind of fine snowflakes buzzed around the streetlamp like a swarm of summer flies.

She opened the window and leaned out to grab the strap that held the shutter in place. Shards of ice stung her face and the wind howled in her ears.

It took some effort to secure the shutter and when she turned back into the room, Bruno was standing in the doorway like a ghost. He was wearing a t-shirt and pyjama bottoms and shivered with cold from the icy blast. His eyes were open but unseeing and he seemed unaware of her presence. Her brother had often wandered in his sleep with no idea of where he was and no memory of having done so in the morning. She recalled her mother ordering him back to bed, murmuring soothingly as she steered him back to the room they shared, and her child's fear of the zombie who'd usurped her brother. Her mother had chided her when she repeated what someone at school had said about those who walked in their sleep being unquiet in their souls.

She went over to Bruno, took him by the arm and turned him round in the direction he had come. His body felt thin and fragile through his t-shirt and he stared at her without recognition, muttering something inaudible, but made no resistance. As they entered his room a gust of wind threw a handful of ice flakes against the glass pane with a sharp rattle. He shivered and gripped her hand as if afraid.

She got him back into bed and pulled the quilt up over him but he continued to hold onto her as she sat there on the edge of the bed, waiting for his breathing to become regular and to relax his grip. Wearing only pyjamas, she grew colder and colder, until eventually she could stand it no longer and slipped in under the duvet. He sighed without waking and nestled his warm body into hers, without letting go of her hand. She lay quite still, conscious only of the frightened child in an adult's body and the brother who, in her ignorance, she'd shunned.

When she entered the café the following morning, Fatimah was waiting for her.

'What are you doing here so early? Why aren't you in school,' Eli asked.

'It's a holiday. I get bored at home, and Kamal said you needed cheering up.'

'He did?'

'Does Bruno make you sad?'

It was remarkable how sharp the child was.

'In a way. I don't know what to do with him.'

She was tempted to confide in someone, but Fatimah was too young.

'I liked him. Is he bad?'

'Not bad. Troubled. They're not the same. Anyway we've got customers.'

When she returned home she found a note from Bruno on the kitchen table, saying he'd be late back as he was meeting some friends after work. Initially she felt a sense of relief. Perhaps at last he was making a life for himself. But as the time of his curfew came and went, she grew restless. It was typical that just when things seemed to be improving, he pulled another of his stunts.

After what seemed like hours, she heard noises on the staircase. She went to the door and opened it a crack, but it was the people who lived on the floor below. She shut the door again, went to the bathroom and ran a bath. She lay there soaking for a while until the water grew cold, then dried herself and got into bed. She tried to read, breaking off every few minutes when she thought she heard his key in the door. At last she heard it open and close. Stumbling footsteps made their way down the hall to the kitchen. Barely able to contain her fury, she got out of bed.

The sight of him silenced her. He was sitting at the kitchen table, his cheeks and forehead criss-crossed with a network of fine lines from which the blood had mostly dried. He looked up and grinned at her drunkenly.

'Like my tattoo?'

'It's grotesque! Where the hell did you get it?'

'It's called "Eastern promise"! Some Turkish guys gave it me. Friends of yours probably.'

'What are you talking about?'

'They don't much like us Germans.'

'You must have done something to provoke them.'

He grinned sheepishly. 'All the fault of your little friend, I'm afraid!'

'Who? Fatimah?'

He nodded.

'She wasn't there, was she?'

He shook his head.

'Thank God!'

'They claimed I lured her to the flat with gifts.' He placed his finger on his nose in a knowing gesture. 'Bad intentions, you see!'

'Surely you told them that wasn't true. She was sent by her father to deliver my wages.'

'Dear Eli! How naïve you are! You think they'd have believed me?'

She felt sick.

'You'd better go and wash your face before you get blood poisoning,' she said wearily. 'There's some antiseptic in the bathroom cabinet.'

He got up obediently and left the room, lurching slightly. She pictured a group of vengeful youths, waiting to grab him then holding him down, relishing his fear as one of them wielded a razor.

When he returned she went over to take a closer look at his cuts. They weren't deep, more like scratches to which here and there encrusted blood still adhered, but they were probably enough to cause scarring.

'Shall I call a doctor?'

She was sure he must be in pain. He shook his head.

She made sweet tea and handed him the mug together with a couple of aspirin. She tried to think if she'd ever let slip to Fatimah that Bruno was on probation, though she was pretty sure she hadn't. It wouldn't take much for her brothers to find out he'd been associated with the far right, in which case he'd be an easy target and the whole thing was her fault.

'You can't go on like this, Bruno. Maybe this time you're not to blame. But things have got to change.'

'And what exactly do you suggest?' He looked at her directly. 'You think I went looking for a fight?'

'I'm not saying that.' She sighed. 'God, it's all such a mess!'

She knew nothing of life on the streets for a young man without friends or allies, whom no one wanted, not even his own parents. What advice could she offer?

'What I don't understand is what possessed you to get mixed up with those fascist thugs in the first place?'

She half expected him to get up and leave the room. Instead he frowned as though in thought, and after a pause looked up at her.

'How many reasons do you want? Because they're everything my father hates. Because he never tried to hide his contempt for the one person I cared about and who cared about me and showed it. Because I hate this country turning into some foreign shithole with a bunch of fanatics who're against everything we stand for…'

'Hardly reasons for smashing up Jewish graves!'

'OK. That wasn't a good move.'

'So was any of it worth it?'

He thought for a moment then grinned. 'The music was good! There was another pause before he went on, 'People do things. My father, no doubt you'd say, had his reasons for joining the Baader-Meinhof lot. Was he justified?'

'He wasn't part of them. His girlfriend was.'

'If that's what you want to believe. Anyway, the answer to your question is no. It wasn't worth it. But that doesn't mean I'm rejoining the fold. The prodigal son's not come home. Just working out his probation.'

She got up. 'I'm going to bed.'

'Go ahead. I shan't burn the house down.'

In a couple of days Bruno's scars were healing well, though they would still be visible when Gunter returned. Looking back all she saw was the naïve vanity of her belief she could show him a more positive way of life. Everything he cared about, including his music, she found abhorrent, not to mention his revolting politics. And no doubt he'd known all along her sole motive was to ingratiate herself with his father. No wonder he was cynical.

Yet there'd been moments when they'd seemed to grow closer, when she'd even felt a fleeting affection. The worst thing was that things weren't likely to improve when Gunter returned, especially if he were tempted to play the heavy father. Being a parent meant subordinating one's own desires to an impossible degree, as Merline had found. Torn between her son and her lover and guilty of farming him out whenever she got the chance to be with Rilke, it was not surprising Balthus had grown increasingly difficult. At least he'd found a way of expressing his pent-up anger in his art, whereas so far Bruno's only outlet had been criminal activity.

Against her better instincts, she decided to search Bruno's room. The curtains were still drawn and the room was stuffy but surprisingly neat. The shelves and desk were almost bare and his personal possessions pathetically few – a couple of battered model cars, relics from childhood, some video games and books, two postcards from his mother in Greece, a poster for a heavy metal band stuck up with Blu-Tack above his bed and beside it some photos of his own band. Apart from that there were his guitar, his Walkman and his clothes. It reminded her of a hotel room where one makes a slightly extended stay, and nothing suggested the slightest attempt to make the place home.

She was about to leave the room, when she caught sight of something under the bed. She knelt down and pulled out a battered suitcase. Inside was a large brown envelope full of old letters. She read one or two of the signatures, mostly his mother and someone who signed himself Big Opa. She glanced at one of these, dated October 3rd 1984. It consisted of a hand-drawn series of cartoons, accomplished drawings of heroes in battle fighting off monsters, comically exaggerated with captions. They must have delighted a seven-year-old boy.

Feeling around the base of the suitcase her fingers closed on something else. It was one of her own Balthus volumes. The corners of some of the pages had been turned down:

'The Room', 'Thérèse Dreaming', 'The Window' and 'The Guitar Lesson', dismissed earlier by Bruno as pornography. In the first two pictures an adolescent girl lay sprawled provocatively in a state of semi-naked abandonment, watched over by the malign gaze of an oversized cat. The other two were even more sexually explicit. In 'The Window' the young woman leans perilously back through the window frame, one breast exposed and an arm raised to ward off her unseen attacker. In 'The Guitar Lesson' a girl lies across the lap of a fierce-looking older woman, who fingers her like a musical instrument. In both pictures the viewer is made to share the coldly voyeuristic eye of the painter and in this way becomes complicit with the sadistic power of his vision. Eli stuffed everything back into the case, pushed it under the bed and left the room.

Bruno's theft intrigued her. She would have liked to repeat to him what Balthus had said during their interview in Paris, that his paintings were part of a long tradition whose violent subject matter was wrapped up in classical or religious themes, whereas in his own work the domestic context made it all the more shocking. She pictured him hearing her out, head on one side, inscrutable as one of Balthus' cats.

That evening when he returned from work, she searched for some casual way to introduce the subject of the pictures. She couldn't confess to having searched his room or whatever shred of trust remained would be destroyed. In the event it was Bruno himself who provided the opening. They were eating supper and he seemed in an unusually chatty mood.

'How's the article going?'

'Slowly.'

'What will you do when you've finished that?'

'Maybe I'll write a novel.'

It was the first time she'd said it out loud.

'What will that be about?'

'I haven't decided.' It wasn't true but she didn't feel like discussing it with Bruno.

'I read what you've done so far.'

'Did it interest you?'

'The analysis of the paintings is OK. All the biographical stuff says is that for someone who started off pretty poor, he ends up a successful painter worth millions.'

'He doesn't want anything known about his life. That way he can build up his own myth.'

'You admire him for his paintings, but you blame him for his success.'

'No, I blame him for lying and denying who he is.'

'So he invented a better life for himself. What's so bad about that?'

'It's a fantasy. He's got about as much right to a title as you or I. That's why half his friends broke off with him.'

'It didn't make him a worse painter. And why shouldn't he be called "Count" if he lives like one? Half the counts in the world have bought their titles.'

She got up and took her plate to the sink. 'Maybe if you were a Jew during the Second World War it made sense to deny who you were. But to continue to deny your Jewish heritage and to replace your family with a bunch of fictitious noble ancestors is despicable!'

'So he invented his own utopia!'

'Like Michael Jackson turning himself white and living in Neverland! It's insane.'

'It didn't stop him singing and dancing his heart out. Maybe that's what it takes to be a great artist.'

'Rilke once said all he'd ever known as a child were the dungeons in the castle of love. D'you think that's what made him a great poet?'

He shrugged. 'If he got himself out of the castle maybe it did.'

'OK! Suffering makes you strong, even wise. But not if all it's about is feeling wronged. That shrivels you up, makes you angry and bitter. Like your fascist pals, who waste their energy blaming others. Such people can never be great artists.'

'What about Ezra Pound? He was a fascist and he's my mother's favourite poet.'

'His case is a more complex... I'm sorry. I'm exhausted. Let's talk some more tomorrow.'

But he wasn't giving up. 'You mean you've run out of arguments! You criticise Balthus, but you haven't a bad word to say about Merline, who had no feelings for anyone but her beloved Rilke.'

'Perhaps if, like him, she'd sacrificed those she cared for to art instead of love, you wouldn't be so quick to condemn her!'

'At least art's worth it! It lasts, and it can make you rich. Love's just selfish.'

'So is anything you focus on to the exclusion of all else… If it's art you admire, you should be more understanding of Gunter!'

'Filmmaking's not art.'

'Oh, really?'

'Well, sometimes it is, in the cinema. Gunter makes stuff for TV, seen once and then forgotten.'

His reply stung her. 'So you despise journalists, like you despise critics?'

'It's a living. It's just not art.'

'And you want to be an artist?' She was unable to keep the sarcasm out of her voice.

'D'you find that so despicable?'

She'd touched a nerve. He got up.

'I'm off to bed,' he said shortly, and left the room.

The following morning she slept later than usual after a disturbed night of dreams. There was no sign of Bruno and, still bruised from last night's confrontation, she felt relieved. As it was Sunday and he wasn't due at work she assumed he was still sleeping. But when he hadn't appeared by midday, she went to his room, knocked and cautiously opened the door a few inches. The bed was neatly made and his belongings gone, including the suitcase under his bed. He must have left in the night and she'd heard nothing.

Her first reaction was panic. Gunter was due home in a few days and how would she explain it if Bruno hadn't returned? They'd had a bit of an argument but that didn't mean she'd driven him out. They'd even started to talk and she'd felt hopeful he was ready to make some important changes in his troubled life. It had been a difficult time for her too, stirring up forgotten fragments of memory, such as her grandparents being forced to flee the home of which they'd scarcely spoken, and whose ghosts, like Merline's, still walked these streets.

Gunter returned in fine form, eager to be with her and to welcome his son. When she told him Bruno had left and she wasn't sure when he'd be back, after an initial moment of disappointment he laughed and said he wasn't all that surprised. Such behaviour was typical and no doubt he'd show up again in a day or so. He was full of his Africa trip and what terrific footage they'd brought back with them, which he felt sure would make a fascinating film. They spent the weekend in bed, making love with all the passion of their early days, something that wouldn't have been possible with Bruno in the flat.

There was no word during the following week but on Sunday, when they were enjoying a late breakfast still in their pyjamas, they heard the sound of a key in the door and footsteps crossing the hall. The kitchen door opened and there stood Bruno. Gunter got up and went over to him, arms spread wide.

'Well! You took your time!'

Bruno rested for a moment in his embrace, before pulling away. 'Any coffee left?' he said and sat down at the table.

'Help yourself.'

Gunter reached for a mug from the shelf, placed it in front of him and resumed his seat.

'D'you want scrambled eggs? They won't take a minute,' Eli asked.

'No, thanks.'

'Toast then?'

'OK.'

She got up and put two slices in the toaster. She knew she was fussing and that he'd only agreed to be polite.

He poured himself some coffee. 'So how was Africa?'

'Inspirational, and tough! Nothing is like you imagine. The landscape is staggering and the people delightful but with little sense of how to help themselves out of poverty. There's a beauty and diversity quite different from all the horror stories we hear. Of course colonialism's left a bitter legacy... What about you? Still at that bloody supermarket?'

'I've only got three more weeks. Then I finish my probation.'

'Well, that's good news! So what then?'

'I've no definite plans.'

Eli placed the toast in front of him. She tried to signal to Gunter to go easy but couldn't catch his eye.

'Now you're back, we need to sit down and have a good talk. You know I'll do whatever I can.'

'I know, Dad.'

There was a short silence before Gunter plunged on. 'Eli told me how disappointed you were not to be travelling with the band. I understand how you feel, but there must be other groups.'

'Not many who are any good.'

Eli pushed a plate of ham and cheese in Bruno's direction in an attempt to create a diversion. Gunter's questioning was in danger of becoming an interrogation.

'D'you still want to be a musician?' he continued.

'I'm thinking of art school.'

'Well, that's great! Your mum'll be thrilled! Have you had any time to build up a portfolio?'

'Like I said, I haven't entirely decided.'

'We must go over the options… I've been looking forward so much to being back with you both. And as soon as we've got a rough cut, I'd like you to take a look at the film.'

His warm smile encompassed them both and she saw the frozen look that passed across Bruno's face.

'Once you've settled back in, maybe we can go somewhere for lunch.' He turned to Eli. 'What about that Russian place in Prenzlauer Berg?'

Bruno intervened. 'I'm not actually staying. I just came to say hi.' His tone was evasive.

'OK. Dinner. If not tonight, tomorrow?'

'I mean I'm living somewhere else.'

Gunter's shock and hurt were written on his face. 'Where?'

'Does it matter?'

'Of course it bloody matters! You've been living here for a month, then I come home and you leave.'

Bruno pushed his chair away from the table. 'I'm sorry. It's just not going to work.'

'At least tell me what's going on,' Gunter said, making a deliberate effort to appear calm.

'I need some space to think things over.'

'OK! You think I'm going to start lecturing you on your lifestyle? That's over as far as I'm concerned. I promise you.'

'It's not that.'

'Then what? If I've been a bit full on, it's because I'm just so thrilled to see you.'

'I know.'

Looking thoroughly miserable, Bruno got up from the table. 'I'll see you both around.'

They listened to his footsteps receding down the hall. As the front door closed behind him, Gunter gave a groan and buried his head in his arms. Eli went over to him and rested her hands on his shoulders, half expecting him to shake her off but he made no move.

Bruno didn't return, even for a visit. Occasionally he called when presumably he knew they wouldn't be in and left a brief message on the answerphone, saying he was doing fine and not to worry but giving no further details. He was eighteen and free to go wherever he wanted without his parents' consent, and since no one in Berlin ever seemed to run into him they assumed he'd gone abroad. One old friend claimed to have seen him queuing for a plane to New York at Frankfurt airport and Malgorzata, who had moved to Greece, eventually received a typed postcard with a Canadian stamp that said, 'Doing fine. Hope you are too. B.'

'He needed to escape if he was ever going to get himself into a better place,' Eli said.

'As long as you don't mean heaven!' Gunter retorted with rare sarcasm. 'Wherever he is, I drove him away. I've done it all his life!'

'He's not a kid any more. You've got to stop blaming yourself.'

'All I know is, you don't free yourself by running away!'

'Sometimes you do! Anyway, he'll probably stage a comeback, or we'll read about him in the newspaper grown rich and successful.'

She was doing her best to lighten the tone.

'Hah! Becoming a criminal's the only way he'll achieve that.'

Gunter's gloom, together with the grey Berlin skies, at times made her ready to pack her bags for London and the comforting trivia of her former life. Work was what mattered, and perhaps in London she'd find less distraction and more inspiration. She thought of Merline's return to Paris and her studio at 15 Rue Malebranche, days filled with the scents of charcoal and oil paint, and in the evening friends gathered around her table for the delicious meals she'd rustle up in her small kitchen. There'd be conversation and laughter and music. When the mood took her, she'd get up and dance, swaying her strong body to the rhythm, joined perhaps by one of the younger men who, like herself, found it impossible to remain still. Sometimes she'd catch sight of herself in the mirror and like the face she saw.

Eli stayed in Berlin. It was where she felt at home, at least more than anywhere else, and she loved Gunter. She did her best to discover more about her grandparents' lives in the city, and tracked down their last address from an old town register. It was a house in Charlottenburg, not far from where Malgorzata had lived, but unlike hers, rebuilt after the bombing. On the pavement outside there were studs put in by the Bundestag to mark the seizure of Jews by Nazis, and at the end of the street a synagogue guarded by armed policemen. It pleased her to know where they'd lived and that more than sixty years later her feet trod pavements they too had walked.

Just before Christmas she submitted her article on Balthus to her editor in London, who wrote back saying he found her ideas interesting, but too many references of a speculative nature to his personal life made it impossible to publish it in its present form. It was the reaction she'd predicted and confirmed what she already knew, that as long as Balthus was alive the gagging order would remain, preventing any serious analysis of his work, at least of the kind that interested her.

Epilogue

Berlin, 2000–2001

Eli took a job assisting one of the curators at the Akademie der Künste. Together with the offers she received from various German publications to write on different painters, it enabled her to earn a small independent living and to feel less of a passenger and more of a partner in the life she and Gunter shared. But still the desire to write something about Merline preoccupied her. The problem was how to tell her story. She imagined some kind of running conversation between the two of them across their different time zones. She might also include an encounter with her grandparents in 1920s Berlin. The key thing was to show how Merline's work as an artist had remained the constant throughout her life, offering salvation from the despair that overwhelmed her at Rilke's death. A portrait of him she'd made in 1923 when they were at Muzot, in which every stroke of her pencil was a telling expression of her love, was in Eli's view one of several exceptional pieces that left no doubt of her standing as a painter. Yet like so many other female artists she'd gone unnoticed, and much of her work appeared to be lost.

Writing a piece of fiction, however, would take her into unknown territory, reviving the ghost of that nagging critic who in her student days had persuaded her she lacked the talent to become an artist. Now he was back, peering over her shoulder and demanding by what right she was ready to court failure and humiliation by adding to that mountain of excess words already in existence. All she could do was block her ears and do her best not to listen.

Then one bright winter morning she woke feeling queasy and exhausted despite a good night's sleep and, when the feeling persisted and her breasts became sore and swollen, she bought a pregnancy test and the world fell about her ears. Just as she'd made up her mind to write, fate played such an underhand trick. Soon the hormonal onslaught would take over her body, consume her creative will and turn her brains to mush, putting paid to all intellectual endeavour. And what would Gunter say to sleepless nights he believed done with forever and another pram in the hall?

But despite everything her spirits rose with each passing day and she was filled with energy. She told herself that as long as she remained healthy for the next eight months the womb was the safest place for a child, providing its every need.

Looked at rationally, eight months should be long enough to finish an outline or even a first draft of a short novel. It would focus her efforts and act as an incentive.

Gunter observed her with growing curiosity.

'I thought you'd decided to give up journalism?' he said, finding her still at her desk when he arrived home.

'Yes, for now. I'm enjoying the freedom to write what I want.'

'Good for you! And this time no deadline!'

'Only one I set myself.'

'I envy you! How about a glass of wine while I make supper?'

A few days of cold sunshine, though it was still only February, gave promise of an early spring. After an enthusiastic reception for his Africa documentary Gunter was preparing another, this time to be shot in Eastern Europe. For the first time in a long while he was enjoying whole nights of restful sleep and she was loath to disturb him with news of the coming child. Sometimes at the end of the working day they met up for a drink or a meal. They avoided Mitte that, with its new bars and fancy restaurants, was relentlessly transforming itself into the fashionable centre of the fledgling capital, preferring to seek out places where one could sit over a plate of wurst and a glass of red without paying extortionate prices or being hassled to free up the table. But when a new French film in its original language was advertised at a small arts cinema in the beautifully restored courtyard of Hackesche Höfe, they arranged to meet there before the show.

Eli arrived first at the restaurant they'd agreed on and chose a table next to the old-fashioned tiled stove, as far as possible from a cluster of defiant cigar smokers. A red velvet curtain covered the entrance to keep out the draught and cut glass lamps gave the place an antique glamour. As she opened the newspaper she'd picked up at the door and began to flick through it, a headline on an inside page caught her attention. It read:

'DEATH OF THE ARTIST BALTHUS, AGED 92. The celebrated painter, Count Balthasar Klossowski de Rola, one of the most controversial artists of the twentieth century, died peacefully today at his home in Switzerland. Famous for being the painter about whom nothing is known, most of his work is in the hands of wealthy collectors who regard him as a rare genius. Others, however, consider his paintings to be little more than a sophisticated form of pornography.'

The date at the top of the page said February 18th, ten days before his elusive leap day birthday.

A feeling as though a light had gone out, leaving the world a darker, drearier place, swept over her. She recalled her last sight of him in Paris, an old man full of life turning himself by sleight of hand into the youth he'd once been. Now he was gone. The circle closed, uniting the end of life with its beginning. His secrets would be laid bare and his critics free to judge him according to the artistic values of the day. It was unlikely any of it would affect his reputation or the value of his paintings, and none of it would make the least difference to the lasting value of his work.

She was contemplating these things when Gunter entered the restaurant. The sudden sight of him never failed to arouse a surge of love, and she waved to attract his attention. When he bent down to kiss her, his face was cold and he smelled faintly of wood smoke.

'You look serious. What are you reading?' he said as he took his seat.

'A death notice… I ordered you a glass of red. I hope we've got time to eat before the film. I'm starving.'

He checked his watch. 'If the service isn't too slow.' He reached for her hand. 'You're cold!' he exclaimed, rubbing it between his own.

'Cold hand, warm heart!'

'I hope so.'

The waiter came. He chose goose and red cabbage with dumplings, whilst she settled on chicken soup.

'I thought you were starving?'

'It's what I fancy. My grandmother's cure for all ills!'

'Have you got ills?'

'On the contrary.'

He took off his coat and placed it under his chair. 'Whose death were you reading about?'

'Balthus. Just before his ninety-third birthday.'

'Not exactly a surprise then! Now you'll be free to write what you want.'

'Yes, but it's too late. I've moved on.'

Their food came and they concentrated on eating.

'At least it means he can't object to the novel you're writing,' Gunter said between mouthfuls. 'How's it going, by the way?'

'I hope to have a first draft in the next few months. Then I'll see.' She paused. 'D'you think life's just a rollercoaster or we decide things for ourselves?'

'I favour the rollercoaster theory. One can resist, but it's best to go with it.'

'Balthus did his best to create his own reality, though in the end I doubt he changed much. Just imagined he did.'

'At least he wasn't a fatalist!'

'Isn't going with the rollercoaster being a fatalist?'

He smiled. 'It depends how you enjoy the ride.'

They left the restaurant, walking arm in arm through the courtyard of Hackesche Höfe. He rested his cheek against her hair. 'You always smell so nice!'

'And if I smelt bad?'

He laughed and pressed her to him. 'I doubt I'd feel differently!'

The cinema was full and they went to their usual place near the front. They both hated sitting at the back and having to gaze at the screen over a sea of heads, surrounded by the rustle of sweet papers and stench of popcorn. The film was enjoyable, though in Gunter's opinion not quite up to the director's previous one. They stood up as the last of the credits rolled and struggled into their coats, preparing to join the crowd shuffling its way up the aisle.

As they neared the exit, Eli's glance drifted over the back rows of the auditorium. They were empty except for four young men, waiting no doubt for the crowd to thin before making their move. They looked like students and their confident voices gave the impression of being cocooned within their own special world. On closer view one of them was older than the others, though from his carefully maintained appearance the difference wasn't immediately apparent. Eli's gaze moved from him to the young man at his side and she did a double take. At first she couldn't believe her eyes but as she looked again there could be no doubt. It was Bruno.

His appearance was completely different from when she'd last seen him. His half-outgrown crew cut was now a dark tousled bob reaching almost to his shoulders, and his air of confidence was entirely new. He was dressed casually in jeans and a battered leather jacket. As she watched he got up and wound a scarf several times about his neck. His gaze swept over the crowded aisle and she shrank into herself, quickly looking away. She was pretty sure he hadn't seen them. She glanced at Gunter, but he seemed unaware of the young men.

They were gathering up their belongings and starting to make their way towards the aisle. In a few seconds their paths would cross. She tightened her grip on Gunter's arm and gestured with her head towards them. She heard his sharp intake of breath and felt the muscles of his arm tighten. Preoccupied with each other, the little group were oblivious to the world.

Gunter put his hand into the small of her back and propelled her forwards so that she trod on the heels of the person in front and almost tripped. They pushed their way through clusters of people hanging about the foyer until they found themselves outside in the square.

'D'you think he saw us?' she asked, breathless.

'God knows!'

He steered her away from the entrance to where they could watch the people coming out. She wondered if he was thinking of his encounter with Jana at that cinema in London long ago and her refusal to acknowledge him.

Bruno was almost the last to exit. He stood with his friends in the square, still engaged in animated conversation. Gunter observed them but made no move. Eventually they walked to the entrance of the courtyard and out onto the street. Gunter and Eli followed, watching as they took their leave of one another. Two of them unlocked bicycles from a stand on the pavement, whilst Bruno and the older man turned in the other direction to where an old Mercedes convertible was parked. The older man produced keys and unlocked the car. Gunter paused a few metres away.

'Speak to him! They'll drive off,' Eli hissed.

Bruno got into the passenger seat as the engine purred to life. The car started to manoeuvre its way out of its tight parking space. At any second they'd be gone.

Suddenly Gunter ran forward and rapped on the passenger window. He saw through the glass the look of astonishment on Bruno's face as he recognised him, then wound down the window.

'Hey, Dad! What're you doing here?'

Fighting his inclination to fire off a volley of questions and reproaches, Gunter replied, 'We've been to the cinema, like you.'

'I'm just back from Canada. I was there two years, working for a print maker.'

'So you're home now?'

'I'm enrolled at the Art Academy.'

'Sorry, Bruno, but we need to get going,' his companion interrupted.

'When will I see you?' Gunter demanded, his hand still gripping the window frame.

'I'll call you. I was going to anyway. Same number?'

'Yes. The same. I'll be waiting.'

Bruno leaned his head out of the window to wave to Eli, who waved back as the Mercedes pulled out of the parking space, forcing Gunter to step back onto the pavement. He stood watching the car as it took off up the street, gathering speed until it was lost to sight. Eli stepped forward and took his arm.

'Couldn't that bastard have hung on two more minutes?' His voice was rough with emotion.

'At least you got to speak to him. Let's go somewhere and get a drink.'

They walked for a while in silence. Eventually he said, 'He looks like a bloody gigolo!'

'Come on! He looks like an art student!'

'He won't call. He's lost to me!'

Suddenly she felt impatient. 'He's not lost unless you close the door on him. Your disapproval is what he's fought all his life.'

He glanced at her as if about to reply, then thought better of it.

'Why can't you just accept him for what he is? It's obvious he's no longer just that stupid kid.'

'So what new stupidity is he involved with?'

She gave a snort of frustration. 'There's no point talking to you in this mood. You paint everything in the worst possible light!'

After a pause he said in a flat voice, 'My mother was an unforgiving, judgemental woman. I swore I'd never be like her and I end up the same.'

'If he can change, so can you.'

'I'm not sure I trust myself any more.'

'That's ridiculous.'

'Maybe.'

He frowned and took her arm. 'At least I've got you here to remind me!'

Instead of a bar they returned to the apartment. Eli made tea and set the vodka bottle beside it on the kitchen table. After the initial shock, Bruno's transformation had not surprised her. Even if it was just another of the identities he assumed while looking for a fit, it was a step up from the last.

Gunter poured a slug of vodka into his cup. Seeing his son had forced him to relinquish the hope he'd clung to that all he had to do was to await the prodigal's return. Worst of all, the feelings of hurt and anger aroused by his son's rejection threatened his sense of himself as a tolerant individual.

'I feel as if I've unwittingly reared a cuckoo in my nest, assuming he was one of my own species. Perhaps if I'd understood Bruno better, I'd have behaved differently.'

'I doubt he knows himself what species he is. It may take him a lifetime.'

'If I was a Buddhist, I might find that comforting… As it is, it means I'll be dead before he finds out.' He was silent for a moment. 'You think your love for your child is unconditional. Then when things go wrong, you ask yourself what that love really amounts to.'

'Love's still love, even if it's critical. Letting Bruno go doesn't mean cutting him off.'

'I wonder if we have anything in common?' He shook his head wearily.

'Perhaps that's what loving a child is. Accepting the stranger they always were.'

He looked up at her. 'Can you love a stranger?'

'I love you!'

He reached across the table and took her hands.

Later that night, as the birds began their dawn chorus, Gunter said softly, 'Are you awake?'

'I am now.'

She turned to face him.

'I want to say how sorry I am for these last four years. I know how hard they've been for you.'

She hesitated. 'There's something I've been wanting to tell you.'

She felt him stiffen as if in anticipation of a blow. 'I'm pregnant. It's not perfect timing and I didn't plan it. But now it's here, I want this child.'

There was a pause, in which she heard his slow release of breath.

'And your novel?' His voice was strange, as though speaking cost him effort.

'Like I said, I'll do a first draft. After that I guess it'll have to go on hold for a while.'

'And you're happy with that?'

'Yes.'

It was still too dark for her to make out his expression.

'Well, I think it's wonderful news!'

She peered closer, trying to see his face in the grey dawn light. 'Really? You're happy to be a father again?'

'I couldn't be more delighted! Perhaps second time around I'll make a better job of it.'

'And if it turns out to be another cuckoo?'

'It'll have Bruno to turn to. Anyway, cuckoo or not I promise you I'll love her.'

'Her?'

'Her, him! Whoever!'

A couple of months before her child was due, Eli was sent to catalogue some of the paintings stored in the basement of the Akademie der Künste, and to her astonished delight she came across the portrait of 'Baladine Dancing' from the exhibition five years ago. Its owner must either have failed to collect it or considered it too insignificant to be worth the bother. Each day she went down to the basement to eat her lunchtime sandwich. Seated on a packing crate, she stared at the portrait until she knew every detail of it by heart with an intimacy that had no need of words. Before her eyes the young girl in the picture metamorphosed into the woman she was to become, undiminished by hardship or rejection.

One day the curator asked her out of curiosity where she disappeared to each day.

'The painting was done by her brother, Eugen Spiro, a Secessionist painter of the period. It's charming but not held in great esteem,' he replied when she told him.

'It's not so much the painting that intrigues me as the girl herself.'

Dancer Baladine Klossowska
© Eugen Spiro / Lebrecht Music & Arts

'She is indeed full of life. The owner, I believe, was a family friend but died soon after the exhibition. No one else has come to collect it so here she stays. If I recall correctly, a dossier was delivered with it. I'll look it out for you.'

She thanked him, and when she arrived at the museum the following morning the file was waiting on her desk.

She went eagerly through its contents, searching for anything of interest. The documents were mainly bills of sale, for the portrait itself, two other pictures, and some drawings of Merline's. There was also a lease agreement for her studio in Paris. Eli could scarcely contain her excitement. The bills of sale might enable her to track down some of her original work.

In the depths of the file was an envelope. Nothing was written on it but inside was a sheet of paper, crumpled as though folded and refolded many times. She smoothed it flat, holding her breath as she gazed at the bold, hastily executed handwriting that covered the page. At the bottom was a signature, 'Merline'. She ran her finger over the letters, feeling the tiny bumps where the nib had caught in the grain of the paper, sending out fine spatters of ink. As she read the words written on the page, she felt a shock as though a bolt of energy passed through her.

The letter was dated March 1927, three months after Rilke's death:

My dearest love,

You are gone, but your presence gives life to each grim day with the glorious fire of your being. Like the Old Testament widow who found always a little precious oil left in her cruz, your light glimmers in my long darkness. Love does not die. It lasts as long as life itself, though I cry out my fury to the indifferent heavens.

If I had borne you the child I begged for there might be some comfort now, a living link to survive us both. But for you a child was just another burden to add to all those that consumed you. Your gift to the world was your precious words and they will be your legacy. You have no need of others.

But I am empty, René. My heart, womb and soul are withered and dry. The most precious memories are as fragile as mayflies, and nothing endures to carry with me into the desert of the years to come. You will say that the drawings I made of you are our children, that I should not demand more. And, you are right! How often did you tell Balthus his riches are his talents – he has no need of others. Oh, how wise you are, René!

Your voice speaks to me now as you hold my head between your two hands, and I must heed it. The time for loving, you say, is over. It is the time for work, which shall be my reward. Dearest René! How well I know your words come from the wisdom of your tender heart! I am not ungrateful. I will summon all my strength and you will see as you look down from your lofty cloud, I am not weak, my darling. I will live and make you proud!

Merline

Eli rested her hand holding the letter on her swollen belly and felt the child stir within.

That night as she lay in bed doing her best to find a restful position, her thoughts turned once more to Merline. Rilke might have declared that all he'd ever known were 'the dungeons in the castle of love', but she had climbed up to its battlements and fearlessly cried out her love to the indifferent world below. Perhaps writing a letter that had no chance of reaching its recipient had done something to ease her grief. She must have put it away in a drawer, where it had lain until her studio was cleared out at her death and by some process of synchronicity found its way to her. She couldn't help feeling that Merline had intended it that way.

Eli's Dream

She was walking beside a canal, or perhaps it was a river, the Seine maybe, because she felt an upsurge of joy only Paris could inspire. It was evening and the sky was a wild mix of gold and duck egg blue. Ahead of her was a figure, walking with easy strides. It was dressed in a long, dark coat belted around the waist, neatly laced shoes, and beret pulled low over a bob of thick hair. Despite its androgynous appearance, she could tell it was a woman because of the grace with which it moved.

Afraid she might turn off and be lost amid a tangle of alleyways, Eli quickened her stride. But however much she hurried, the space between them didn't lessen and when she called out, her voice made no sound.

Suddenly, as if by some instinct, the woman paused in her walking and turned in her direction.

Eli cried out in joyous recognition, and the restraining force let go. She ran towards the woman, waiting with outstretched hand, and together they resumed their walk.

Most of the letters quoted in this novel I have freely translated from the French, in the case of Merline from a small, out of print volume I came across in the Senate House Library at London University. One or two I have invented, having grown so accustomed to her voice.

Acknowledgements

Thank you to Rebecca Swift and Aki Schilz at The Literary Consultancy for their invaluable criticism and encouragement, to Loveday Herridge for proof reading with an eye for detail second to none, to Bettina Wilhelm, Barry Devlin, Iro Staebler and Kate Saunders for reading and re-reading, and to Yen Ooi and my wonderful daughter, Hannah Corbett, for making this happen.

About the Author

Photo credit: Jake Corbett

Jane Corbett studied English at Newham College, Cambridge, and is the author of a YA novel *Out of Step*, a volume of modern fairy tales titled *Beasts and Lovers*, and several award-winning screenplays. In the seventies she taught at the progressive Kingsway College, including among her students John Lydon and Timothy Spall. Now, she runs workshops for writers and filmmakers and teaches documentary filmmaking at the National Film and Television School. Her other passions are horse riding, yoga and her grandson. She lives in London with her husband.

www.janecorbett-writer.com